THE GEEK'S GUIDE TO WRITING BL NOVELS IN ENGLISH - YAOI

WRITE, SELF-PUBLISH AND SELL YOUR STEAMY ROMANCE STORIES

PEPI VALDERRAMA

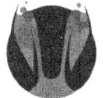

COPYRIGHT

THE GEEK'S GUIDE TO WRITING BL

Write, self-publish and sell your dream Yaoi story

Published by dePepi.com

Copyright (C) 2022 by Pepi Valderrama

This book is licensed for spark your imagination and entertain the idea that you can write Romance too. This book is for your entertainment only and may not be copied and shared unlawfully. Thank you so much for respecting the hard work a fellow writer like you.

Although the book has been written with the most recent examples, please do research of your own since the self-publishing online landscape is changing like lightning. You should always carry out your own research and try to do your best to deliver the best version possible to your readers with the latest information possible.

Thank you for making my dream the inspiration to ignite yours.

CONTENTS

I could write that too!   vii

PART ONE
DISCOVERING

1. What exactly is BL?   3
2. A short history on BL   6
3. It's only BL   10
4. BL, a source of Freedom   12
5. Writing BL is like dating in different shoes   15
6. Choose your BL genre   17
7. Warnings and Tropes   21
8. The role of Author's notes in fan-fiction   28
9. Fan-fiction and Copyright   36

PART TWO
WRITING BL ROMANCE

10. Types of BL characters   41
11. Choose your lead characters   46
12. Create your main character's profile   52
13. Spice up your characters   58
14. Do you need world-building if I'm writing romance?   62
15. Creating a timeline   64
16. Steps that must appear in a BL (Romance) Novel   68
17. The Hero's Journey   71
18. Beginning, Climax and Resolution   76
19. Being an Utter Bastard to your Characters   79
20. Sex and Steam   82
21. Elements of Style   86

PART THREE
SELF-PUBLISHING

22. Where to place your BL novel in the Kindle Store   91
23. Short fiction in the Kindle Store   101
24. Keywords, categories, the feared book description & blurb   104

25. Give your book a price! 107
26. E-books and paperbacks 109
27. Create your amazing cover 111
28. Marketing Romance 114

PART FOUR
EXTRAS

29. Main BL/Yaoi/801 words 121
    About dePepi 135

*To those who dare
pursue their dreams*

I COULD WRITE THAT TOO!

There's a secret about you that's hot an amazing: you love BL stories. You've been reading BL manga, BL novels and fan fiction for years. You're passionate about the drama and steam of the characters in these stories, their struggles and their personalities. And now, you're also thinking: "I could write that too!"

Or perhaps you've been reading BL and secretly writing fan fiction for years and now you're also thinking: "I could self-publish those stories too!"

There's some good news: if you think you can do it, then you can! There's only a bit of planning and practice to throw to the magic cauldron to make it happen. Although there's no big formula on how to realize your dream of becoming the next BL Queen (or King), there's one thing certain: where there's a will there's always a way. In this case: a very steamy one alongside some good writing practice and plotting.

Writing romance stories centered in male couples can be exhilarating. BL, short for boys love, or "yaoi" (the Japanese equivalent as used in the West) are mostly romance stories from the female gaze perspective. And yet, that's changing and fast. In the same way anyone can read BL nowadays, it's also true for creators. You can be one, so can your neighbor, and Steve, your co-worker. (Hi

Steve!) What began as female-gazed is now evolving and getting more interesting.

This is fantastic news since it means that there's room for experimentation and coming up with great stories and ideas. Although the genre has been plagued from the beginning with tropes, now is the time to either subvert them or ditch them forever (especially some negative traditional ones).

You and I are going to explore nice possibilities in writing top-notch BL stories and give them some steam (if you are up for that). We'll also explore how to self-publish and make some residuals from our amazing stories. Yes, darling, we're going to take a look on what to do with that brilliant draft number three, polished and shinny ready to be shared with the world! Here's where Kindle can help us massively.

However, before we go into the nitty-gritty details of all the steps into becoming a badass BL writer, we need to start with some basics.

Although boys love (BL), *yaoi* and slash fiction are often put in the same bag, in Japan all these are slightly different. Even if the line is getting blurred little by little, BL would be "romance" and *yaoi* would be "erotica". Writing BL stories can help you spark the practice of writing and getting more confident while self-publishing your original tales. There's no brainer: the more you write, the better it gets.

BL is often thought to be a genre specifically for manga (Japanese comics). However, it also includes soft novels too. Which is good news for us: writing short novels and long series and then self-publishing them will be the key to your small empire on Kindle Books.

The most important thing to remember is that the biggest thing that will separate you from the authors you love reading is that they wrote a book and published it somehow. So, prepare yourself to sit down and star writing until you get that story out in the world!

THIS BOOK IS FOR YOU IF:

1. You love reading BL Romance.
2. You've been writing some BL fan fiction or stories in your diary or in forums.
3. You have a stash of stories hidden in your computer ready to see the light, but you've been shy about it.
4. You've been thinking about self-publish your stories and maybe make some cash in the process, but don't exactly know how to do it.

PART ONE
DISCOVERING

ONE
WHAT EXACTLY IS BL?

BL saw the light first as *yaoi*, a genre that centers stories in boys love. Although it's usually manga, there are many soft novels out there. BL sits within the romance umbrella, within the LGBTQ+ category within the Kindle Store. In Japan, the market is booming with all sort of books. Meanwhile, in the West, there's also a fair share of LGBTQ+ romance stories too. There's no surprise in discovering that BL is in fact pure romance! There's more romance out there than meets the eye. That last fantasy novel where you were shipping some characters? That's romance too!

Yaoi or 801 is an acronym for 「ヤマなし、オチなし、イミなし」 (*yama nashi, ochi nashi, imi nashi*). It simply means "no climax, no punch line, no sense". It's a general word that nowadays equals to "boys love" (BL), however it is way closer to erotica (very hot steamy romance). Erotica is more centered in the gymnastics of the main characters than the drama and feelings happening in the story. The number 801 in Japanese is also read *yaoi*, where "ya" is number 8, "o" is the zero, and "i" is number 1.

While words might be interchangeable in the West, not so much in Japan. Despite that, what we'll be centering ourselves here is writing good BL soft novels to self-publish in the Kindle Store.

However, if you want to go into the erotica side, please, don't be shy. There's just one rule: try to research if you don't know the arena otherwise you might end with something readers might not connect with or worse, something they might hate.

―――――

Yaoi: acronym that comes from 「**ヤ**マなし、**オ**チなし、**イ**ミなし」(**ya**ma nashi, **o**chi nashi, **i**mi nashi), or "no climax, no punch line, no sense." It refers to stories that without sex wouldn't have any meaning. Hence, they center the focus in the sweaty action. Some fans, however, have re-interpreted the acronym. Instead, they argue it comes from 「**や**めて、**お**尻が**痛**い！」 (**ya**mete, **o**shiri ga **i**tai!), or "stop, my butt hurts!" This ironic statement might be connected to one of the most prevalent tropes in the genre: *romantiziced non-consesual sex*. You'll find out that many stories depict non-consensual sex as precursor of a loving relationship. In Japan, this term is usually left for Doujinshi (fan works). However, it's used as a synonym for BL in the West (which can be quite confusing).

801: is yaoi written with numbers. In Japanese, you can write words with numbers by taking into consideration the pronunciation of the numbers. Eight is "ya" or "hachi," zero can be also an "o" and read as an "o," and one can be "i" or "ichi." It feels like a code, but since you can find this type of word-number play virtually everywhere, anyone can read it.

Bara: 「バラ」, or rose, refers to hyper-sexualized and very graphic yaoi stories. These usually aren't directed to a female audience but to a gay male one. Beware, because "bara" is also used by the gay subculture. Thus, "bara" might only mean "gay culture" as a whole for the Japanese.

Boys Love: 「ボーイスラブ」 or BL 「ビーエル」 is the "umbrella" term for boys love (and *yaoi*) in Japan. This term was first used in 1991 by the magazine *Image* in an effort to use it as an umbrella term at the time. However, it wasn't until 1994 when *Puff* *magazine* started to use it. BL took the market over June which was a word first used to describe such stories.

Shonen-Ai: 「少年愛」 is basically BL. However, stories are more focussed on romance and not sex. Hence, there's a great focus on the feelings and the story. And even if sex is happening in closed doors, the manga will show little of it. Originally, in the 1970s, this referred to stories of androgynous boys inspired by European literature.

June: 「ジュネ」 was a magazine that back in 1978; this word derived from it. However, the stories were a little bit tragic since one of the partners would always die. By the 1990s this word disappeared in favor of the umbrella term of BL (plus the other publishers were happy to change, since June was also the name of the magazine!)

TWO
A SHORT HISTORY ON BL

FROM SHONEN-SHOUSETSU TO SHOUNEN-AI TO YAOI TO BL

What we nowadays understand as *yaoi* had its origins back in the 1970s. However, we can go further back in time to take a look at *Murasaki Shikibu* a novelist of the *Heian Period* who wrote one of the first (if not the first) "soap opera" novel in the world. It was called *Genji Monogatari*, aka The Story of Genji. Her influence touched many in the centuries to come.

In Murasaki's novel, Genji, the main character, had both male and female features. He is an "idealized" version of what men could be. This female-gazed character appeared in a moment in time where "bushido", aka the path of the warrior, would stress and promote a "male without feelings" culture. In this "macho world" Genji was a revolution! (This is not happening at the beginning of the 20th century but during the 10th and 11th!)

Murasaki compares his hero, Prince Genji, to a female when describing him, making him closer to her audience. This influence appeared many centuries later, in 2002 in a film called "Genji: a Thousand-Year Love" (https://asianwiki.com/Genji:_A_Thousand-Year_Love). It's an actress, *Yuuki Amami*, who plays the hero (and not a man!) She was a famous actress of the *Takarazuka Revue*, an all-female musical theater.

So, what does classic literature and the *Takarazuka Revue* Theater has to do with BL? Have you ever read the manga by the father of the medium Osamu Tezuka, called "Princess Knight" (https://en.wikipedia.org/wiki/Princess_Knight)? This is another classic, this time, published in 1953. It depicts a girl dressed as a boy who inherits two hearts: one as a boy and one as a girl. To save the throne of her country, she has to play as a boy. The influence of the *Takarazuka Revue* Theater is obvious. The funny thing is that Takarazuka is a town in Osaka, and Tezuka was born in the area of Osaka. His mother was a great fan of these stories, and these influenced his manga, which in turn would influence BL stories.

In Japan, the manga for women has the characteristic of depicting ambiguous characters where they can be either boys or girls at the same time. These androgynous characters are the heroes in BL stories.

Before the manga for girls, aka *Shojo manga*, appeared in the 1970s, there were tons of novels for girls called *Shojo shousetsu*. These novels date back to the "Flower Tales" of Nobuko Yoshiya (1916 - 1924 * 「花物語」). The main character tends to be a very beautiful girl who suffers a lot and overcomes all types of obstacles (a little bit like chick lit, only a little bit more dramatic). One of these novelists was Mari Mori who took these stories one step further and wrote three novels where the main characters weren't girls, but men professing love to each other. "The Lovers' forest", "I don't go on Sunday", and "The Bed of Withered Leaves" were all a hit that would influence the genre for years.

Mari went to Paris and was thrilled with one novel in particular: "The Picture of Dorian Gray". If you haven't read the novel, please do so, because it'll give you the chills and hopefully give you some creative mojo as happened to Mari. In her novel "The Lovers' Forest" she would create a fantasy world for her readers, in a far away land, creating a nice and enduring escapist story.

This is when *Shounen-Ai* (boys love) would first appear, where stories would depict young men in European setups. The only downfall to these novels is that they all end in tragedy.

Another thing that influenced BL was the sexual revolution of the 1960s, French paintings from Millet and movies like "This Special Friendship" (1964 - https://en.wikipedia.org/wiki/Les_amitiés_particulières_(film)). Authors like Keiko Takemiya, Hagio Moto and Norie Masuyama would end up forming the "Year 24 Group" and become the starting point of BL manga.

The first BL manga was Keiko's "In the Sunroom" published in a special issue of "Shoujo Comics Magazine" in 1970. We follow the story of two beautiful boys who fall in love while living in Europe. And here is where a boom on BL stories rocked the publishing world as it was known until date. The ladies were taking the manga world like a tornado!

Moreover, the idea of "beautiful boys" came also from re-known literature (and crazy) author Yukio Mishima who brought homoeroticism to the table. He posed as a model for the photographer Eiko Hosoe 1961 in a picture called *Barakei* (killed by roses). The word *bara* 「バラ」 would then become the name for gay comics. The first gay magazine as called *Barazoku* and released in 1971.

While in the 1970s the words "boys love" (*shounen-ai*) and June (name of a magazine) was used to describe *yaoi* works at the time, BL (in English) would finally be used as a nice umbrella for the genre. While the main publishing houses would be focussing on mainstream stories, fans would be creating *doujinshi* 「同人誌」 with wild stories. These self-published works included all types of fan fiction. It was so popular that fans would gather around. The first Comiket convention was held in 1975 and it's been a must for fans ever since.

It's around this time that the word *yaoi* appeared. The word was coined by Yasuko Sakata and Akiko Hatsu to describe funny stories with no climax, no point and no meaning. This type of erotica is very steamy.

The mocking flavor of the word did not stop it to overcome *Shounen-Ai* as a genre. By the 1980s series like Patalliro were

A SHORT HISTORY ON BL   9

adapted to TV. However, it was Comiket and *Doujinshi* that would make groups like CLAMP shine and soar during the 1990s and bring BL to the spotlight. While *yaoi* kept being "the western" with few rules, BL would be taken by mainstream and bring it to withering heights.

It wouldn't be a nice tale if there wouldn't be some drama, would it? The *Yaoi* Debate highlighted the shortcomings of the genre. What is *yaoi*? Is it only for women? What about all the rape and misrepresentation of the LGBTQ+ community? Fortunately, from the 2000s stories have been taking more depth and are slowly focusing on having great characters and good plots. However, the debate is still ongoing. Hence, the stress of crafting good characters and a story where tropes are not abused nor misrepresenting a nice community.

 L started as literature, then became comics, and now is returning back to literature again. Good times!

THREE
IT'S ONLY BL

The BL label can be a blessing or a curse. It's like a little bit like the romance label. Without it, you wouldn't find your favorite books. But at the same time, many people don't give the respect to the genre that it deserves. That's one of the main reasons many people prefer writing under a pen-name. Nicknames and other personas might help you at the beginning of your self-published author.

"If you live by the sword, you die by it too". It means that, if we start writing books related to the genre, we might get stuck to them and it might be difficult to present ourselves as serious in front of some eyes. But no one says we can't write different genres and use different nicknames.

The problem with BL (and romance, which is its wider umbrella term and genre), is that many people assume it means just erotica and it might be cheap (not only in price but in contents). What's worse, you might end up making a decent living by selling your romance stories on Kindle Store, Kobo and other platforms, and yet some folk will still think of your success as a lesser one. Stories now are very varied and you can touch as heavy contents and have very intricate contents. Including different degrees of steam. Whatever some people might think, in reality, it doesn't matter as long as you're happy with your path and success.

Humans love to label and it will help us greatly when placing our BL soft novel in the Kindle store. But the label that will help us sell goes beyond BL: is it a fantasy BL romance? Are there some aliens involved? Then it's also sci-fi. Is there any harem inside? Are there some elves or maybe werewolves messing around too? (You get the picture).

Basically, if you write anything with male characters in love thinking that most of your audience is going to be female, you're writing a BL story. If someone comes to you and tells you that what you're writing isn't serious, don't listen to them. There're good and bad BL books out there. Not because you're writing romance it automatically means that you're writing something second class! (So, don't listen to the haters).

FOUR
BL, A SOURCE OF FREEDOM

Writing BL can be therapeutic. Fiction where you create the rules and you imagine you're someone else, explore different relationships or simply rant about your ex can be therapeutic. Writing is always exhilarating, revenge on people who mistreated us in books can be a blessing. However, if you go this way, please remember to not make them too similar to your foes! It might feel amazing while you're writing it, but it can also be a curse if you end up crafting a character too realistically close to your ex!

If you draw from reality inspiration and turn it into steam in a page, if you want to transform a pairing that would never happen into a reality in the pages of your novel, this is the good way to go. However, while writing with heavy inspiration in reality, we need to be nice to ourselves and others. Yes, that includes your readers.

Yaoi or Boys Love (I'll use it here as synonyms) is a great tool to explore yourself and skill up your writing. It can be used to open ourselves and explore ourselves and also to do some self-therapy. Very much like journaling, writing stories can be exhilarating.

You can free your mind from all limits by exploring fan fiction and/or BL. But while this might be super, we need to be aware of others if we're to publish our work online. We need to be nice with ourselves but also with others.

Although the genre might be a source of freedom, the reality is that writing good boys love is actually very tricky. Make sure that you won't fall for "the tropes" in the genre that are negative cliches (there are tons!) Many manga are plagued with tropes. If your favorite author uses them a lot, that doesn't mean that you'll need to do the same. Writing a good story means that refraining to fall into tropes is paramount. Reverting tropes is also amazing, however it's a very difficult thing to do in writing. For that, you'll need a ton of writing (which is cool, because the more you write, the better you'll get).

One of the cool things about *yaoi* is that your characters are equal. The constrains of society can be lifted and you can put both protagonists at the same level, with the same opportunities. Here's the golden opportunity to explore other assets. However, try not to create characters that are too perfect or too idealized. If you want to do something differently, fish from the source to get inspiration and then take this inspiration to write something amazing. Dare to explore and tinker before you find your true writing path.

WRITE, SHARE, BREATH IN

While writing a lot is great, at a certain point you might start thinking about sharing your work online. There's one thing to take into consideration while sharing: criticism. Sooner or later someone is going to trigger you somehow. Breath in: either they're not reasonable or you might be over-reacting. Maybe someone got triggered by your story, or they thought it wasn't nice at all. Instead of shutting them down, try to get a conversation and learn from it. Did something happen in the story that wasn't good or that it could have been misunderstood? Can you fix it?

If instead they're being rude, breath in and erase them (or tell the Admin to help you out). Don't take their criticism too seriously since you could be putting limits into you being a great writer.

Write, share and breath in while taking in feedback. Don't shut people out and learn if the feedback is constructive and how you can use it to your advantage.

Just free your mind and write. Then, write some more.

FIVE
WRITING BL IS LIKE DATING IN DIFFERENT SHOES

One of the big questions is: how much do you want to charm your reader? Well, writing BL is very much like dating your reader. You want your reader to stick around not until the end of the book they're reading, but to fall in love with you so massively that they'll be eager to read all (or most) of your other books.

For that you need to be true to yourself. You can't pretend to be someone you're not because it'll flop. You can't fake your voice nor write a book that it's not your style just because you think it's going to sell. It won't work in so many levels: first, your voice won't ring true, and second, who says that genre will be on the top sellers once you finish your fantastic book?

Also, dating should be fun, shouldn't it? Writing is pretty much the same. If you have fun with what you're writing, then it will show up! Don't take your journey seriously, but just have fun with it and then self-publish when you're happy with the final edit of your draft.

You should be also prepared to write a lot. It's super cool reading all your favorite stories. But it's way harder than you think to put all the words together and plan a great plot that works and that will thrill your soul. It requires some practice.

What's more, there's also a possibility for starting a story and leave it on the way through writing because it doesn't tune with you anymore. It's just fine. If you're not that much into your story anymore, then let it go. Don't force things. Don't just keep writing something because you think you have to finish no matter what.

On the flip side, if you committed to writing a story you're passionate about but are a massive procrastinator, you'll need to make up your mind: do you really want to finish writing that story? If so, you'll need to keep writing and try to do a little bit every day.

Unfortunately, rejection will also happen in the self-publishing arena. In the same way that you might have negative feedback online when you share your fan fiction stories, it might happen that you might find people that won't like your book. Constructive negative feedback is always good because we can take some in and improve. However, if the feedback doesn't add anything: just ignore it and move on.

If you would choose the traditional path for publishing, you'd be exposed to a lot of rejection before you find someone that will publish your book. Let's say it's like a "rite of passage" of sorts. If you stop with the first rejection, you will never see your story published.

Just like dating, you'll meet readers that will be thrilled, and others that won't be that thrilled with your book. Your aim is to charm as many readers as possible so that they're happy when they finish your book and are eager to read more from you.

So, how to charm your reader? Well, we'll talk about it through this book. But basically, it's having fun writing and let it show in your first draft and then remembering to be consistent. Then, make them "have all the feels" along with your main character.

> **to have all the feels*: to feel everything the character is going through, the good, the bad and the evil. You want your audience to love your characters (and hate you're such a bastard for having them go through such an ordeal before they can have their sweetheart!)

SIX
CHOOSE YOUR BL GENRE

The Kindle bookstore is a library with almost endless shelves. So much so, that it's a giant search engine. Exactly! The Kindle Store is not a book store but a humongous search engine! Hence, we need to be super clear about what romance sub-genre will be choosing and how likely we'll hit the top of the chart. We'll be developing this topic deeper later on in this book, but for the time being let's be clear: BL is within the "LGBTQ romance" umbrella, even if it's mostly from a female gaze perspective. It means that you'll be located under romance, then probably under the LGBTQ romance category, and then you can choose another smaller "niche" where people can find your fantastic book.

The good news is that most genres mix and match other genres, and BL shouldn't be different. Before you start having a full idea of your story, decide which genre you want to stick with the most. Do you love vampires? Then, go ahead!

ROMANCE GENRES FOR YOUR BL STORY

Let's be real: romance is a very huge umbrella with many sub-genres that can be mixed (for our delight). However, all have something in common: stories are mostly focussed on love and feelings.

Contemporary romance

The setting happens in our timeline. Even if the town is fictional, as long as if it has our technology, no magic, and the world is like ours, then you're writing a contemporary story.

Within this genre there're other sub-genres like billionaire romance, small-town romance, yakuza, mafia, etc.

Historical romance

When you set up your story in a different time-frame, even if it's just 50 years ago, then you're writing a historical story. For some reason many books happen during the Victorian and Regency era. Someone please explain to me the appeal of that… is it the fashion? (As you guessed, I'm not exactly a fan for those eras…)

Fantasy romance

If there's magic, elves or fantastical creatures around, you're writing fantasy. If you create an alternate world full of treacherous faeries trying to pull apart your main character from his love, then that's a fantasy book. (If you're thinking about Sarah J.Maas and Holly Black, you're in the right path!)

Paranormal romance

Are there vampires or werewolves? Is any of your characters a shapeshifter? Is someone a supernatural creature? Then you're writing a paranormal romance!

Paranormal books have their roots in Gothic stories and might be spooky or not. Although they might have fantasy elements they happen mostly in the ordinary world. (Vampire Diaries anyone?)

Young adult romance

YA is the most lucrative genre of all! Seriously: not only young adults are hooked, but also readers of all ages. But, please take in mind that young adult stories are for ages around 14 to 17 year-olds. That first love when you were young hooks thousands, and for good reason. (Again: Sarah J.Maas anyone?)

New Adult Romance

Or also known as "what happens right after a young adult romance" story. These stories have more steam and more sexually explicit scenes than young adult ones. Ages in this arena go from 18 to 25 years old. Sarah J Maas *A Court of Thorns and Roses* series starts within the umbrella of young adult, and as the characters and the story progresses, it fits perfectly with a new adult audience!

New adult stories are also read by virtually anyone! So don't think that only people in the age-range will be the only ones to read them.

Erotic romance

This is when you have something like a young adult book with all the steam inside. Basically, you find a very compelling story with all the love story and you also get all the sweat and tiny gritty bitty. In erotic romance sex is a must because it's an element part of the story.

Erotica

Erotica is not erotic romance. Erotica focuses primarily in sex and the story is just secondary. This is where you have more "one shots". Those books that your auntie reads before going to sleep? Yeah, might be one of those.

Genre Festa!

Don't worry: there're even more genres out there where you can fit your BL story! (Why is this important? When we'll talk about self-publishing your book and where to place your book this will be super important).

So here you have some other genres. This is not an exhaustive list. In fact, some genres are here to stay while others disappear after some years. Hence, I would choose one of the more-or-less stablished ones to place your steamy story in the most suitable virtual shelf.

Adventure

The main character goes on a quest of sorts (like Bilbo in *The Hobbit* or Bilbo in *The Lord of the Rings*). This adventure might be fictitious or it might be historical, and it can indeed have some romance too. It can also have elements of dystopia or mystery.

Chick Lit

Chick lit tells the daily lives, relationships and adventures of the main character, mostly female. Think about the *Bridget Jones Diary*, for example. It's about dating, romance, fashion, difficult times, weight problems… you name it!

Dystopian

The story happens in a new, alternative or futuristic world where values and society are degraded. There's oppression and terror all over. It usually has some science fiction, romance and conflict. For example, *The Hunger Games* or *The Maze Runner*.

Science Fiction

It's fiction based on an imaginary future where technology is amazing. There might be a lot of space travel, alien civilizations, etc. For example, take *The Cinder, the first of the Lunar Chronicles* by Marissa Meyer.

Steampunk

This genre is a bit tricky since is mostly place within the science fiction umbrella, which would make of it a sub-genre. Whatever the case, it portrays a world were technology and gadgets have ben stuck in the 19th century. It's a type of Victorian Era flavor mixed with science fiction (or even fantasy). Think about the *Mortal Engines* by Philip Reeve.

SEVEN
WARNINGS AND TROPES

You not only need to be nice to yourself, but also with your readers. You might need to think twice about writing about a certain pairing, or need to research a bit before publishing your masterpiece. Whatever the case, there're some do's and don'ts when writing Yaoi.

STAY AWAY FROM NEGATIVE TROPES

Don't use any tropes! (At least, the worse of them all). You can find an extensive list of tropes on TV Tropes (https://tvtropes.org/pmwiki/pmwiki.php/Main/YaoiGenre). There's a very long list; however, try to stay away from the below one like the plague.

The feminized Uke

As you probably already know, the Uke is the "passive" one in the relationship. Ukes can be very active and might be completely in control of the whole relationship, so depicting them as a "school girl" with male organs doesn't make them a favor. That's a very divisive trope and it brings more headaches than anything else. This trope could be associated with femme-phobia. Hence, better avoiding it.

Consider to make your characters round, sound and daring or shy in a natural way. Consider the setting when the action is happening and the personality traits of the character. Don't just make them fall in a trope.

There're no rules in writing. There are not limits in the world you're creating. The trick to make it work is to make it consistent with your characters.

STAY AWAY FROM HOMOPHOBIC AND TRANSPHOBIC STEREOTYPES

Consider researching a type of story before starting to write. It's way easier to write what you know. However, it's also very alluring to venture into the unknown. You can research a bit or ask friends. Just take in mind that everyone is reading *yaoi* these days (and yeah, it might include people of all ages and from different orientations).

For example, while it might look that *seme/uke* (top/bottom – man/woman) is okay, it's in fact a homophobic stereotype that can be both misogynistic and misandristic. Social constructs can be very negative, and trying to continue with those might do more harm that you might think. It's not an innocent thing, at all.

When you write BL please take in mind that straight men are straight men, gay men are gay men, and bisexual men do exist. Bisexuals are not fantasy creatures that only exist in the ether. It stings when you read some writings that erase you. So, don't erase your characters because you might be erasing your audience too! Also, remember to treat trans men as men because they're men.

Furthermore, rape is rape. There's no love at all involve in that. Non-consensual intercourse is just hell. Survivors of rape can be heavily triggered. If you want to still touch the topic, be respectful and realistic. Again: research and be very careful when writing.

Another trope is high male promiscuity. Not all men are obsessed with sex, and not all gay are obsessed with sex. The vast majority of people do have moral compasses and it's very painful reading certain stories out there that make no good for anyone. Don't use "excuse plots" either. Simply speaking, an excuse plot is a plot that's there only to justify something to happen. Excuse plots tend not to add anything to the main story.

YOU DON'T NEED SEX, REALLY

Just sex makes the story "boring". It's just one shot and then it gets forgotten into oblivion. However, if you create a story compelling because of the plot, and the sex is just accessory, people will stick to it like glue. Also, you don't need to heat things up too much, just if you feel comfortable with it. And if you are not feeling too comfortable, just insinuate that something happened. Use the "sexy discretion shot". (A little bit like in the movies in the 50s where you have a couple kissing while traveling in a train, and then the train enters into a tunnel.)

It's better to fade off steam than writing sex awfully.

LEARN ABOUT ANATOMY

It sounds weird but, if you've been reading too many *Omegaverse yaoi*, you should probably check the wikipedia for some anatomy traits. Anuses are not like vaginas at all. Unless your story belongs to an alternate universe, anuses are sensitive and if you don't want to have issues you need to prepare before having anything incoming.

Also, it's a good idea to learn about poses. I don't know how to draw realistically at all (my drawings are mostly big headed cute dollies). However, I have a pretty good idea how bodies work and sometimes we might imagine anatomical scenes that are literally impossible to achieve with our muscles and bones in the real life. Unless one of your characters is a shapeshifter with elastic capabilities, do research how the real deal works or your audience will end up rolling their eyes.

DON'T FORGET PEOPLE IN THEIR 30s, 40s, 50s...

Although many *yaoi* manga is plagued with stories with teens, reality is that readers belong to a vast array of ages. Hence, set up your stories in the full age spectrum depending on the age-range you're targeting with your story. Older characters with problems and falling in love are very alluring too. To be honest, I had my fare share of high-school and I do crave for more.

You have University, your first job, a divorce, finding love in the office... you name it! Just dare to go beyond high-school!

MAKE YOUR AUDIENCE FEEL

Ultimately, the key to success is to make the audience feel what the characters feel. Make them go along with your main character and grow along with him. Be bold and drop on that page all the feelings you can!

TROPES TO ERASE FROM EARTH

Some of the tropes below are to be erased from the face of Earth. Seriously! Here you have some very bad examples:

A TRANS PERSON GOAL IN LIFE IS TO BE LOVED BY A CIS PERSON

That's not the goal of anyone's. So, erase it and never touch it. True, many movies do it, but does doesn't mean that you should apply the trope in your writings.

TRANS WOMEN ARE UNSTABLE

To begin with, trans women are women. Some women show their feelings, others not. And some people, regardless of their gender, might be unstable. But not because someone is a trans women it automatically means that they're unstable.

If you're going to write feminine characters alongside your heroes, don't make of them pools of instability!

THE HOT GIRL WHO IS IN FACT A TRANS WOMEN AND THE CIS MAN FREAKS OUT IN DISGUST

This is one of the most used tropes ever. It's disgusting and it keeps up with violence against trans women. Whatever phobia this expresses, it's harming everyone.

Again, female characters in your story, being main characters or helping ones, have to be consistent and not just balls of cliches!

IN SHORT…

Beware of what you see on the movies and ask yourself if it's okay or not before using it. However, if you don't have first hand experience, the best thing to do is to get informed and ask!

Example: Crimson Spell

Let's take an example of BL (that I love, because I love the drawings, mind you) that is plagued (like many others, not a secret by the way) with tropes. Let's see some of them (it doesn't mean these are bad, it's just an example that we have to be extra careful not to mess things up!)

Black comedy rape

In one of the extras of Crimson Spell, one of the main characters, Vald, goes against some "naughty tentacles". Writing comedy with something as serious as rape is very difficult and can go wrong easily. The background of this trope relies on the idea of men, if manly, won't need to ask for help. Worse, if you're unable to prevent it then it's because you deserve it.

Assault is all about power, not sex. It belittles the survivor so the perpetuator makes you do what they want you to do. The problem with this trope is that it's very difficult to achieve. Before attempting to bend the rules, just practice and ask for feedback from friends. Let them read your story and then ask what they thought about it. This might help decide if you still want to stick with it.

Deus Sex Machina

So, what's the solution for Halvir, one of the main characters, to relax Vald? Going all sexy! So he'll do all types of sex to make the other character relax. You can use this trope to explore sex as a metaphor for something else. However, let's be honest, it's an excuse to put some sex within the plot. If overused, it becomes disruptive to the story.

So, instead of having a Halvir going full Deux Sex Machina on your Vald, try to figure out natural scenes where very hot exchanges happen. Don't just use this trope as an excuse (then you have two tropes, because you'll have an excuse plot too!)

Forceful Kiss

When you force kiss that ends up in steam. The reality is that if someone forces you to kiss them, you'll want to escape, not to kiss them back!

Idealized sex

Halvir and Vald have lots of "idealized sex" together. What about preparing the anus? What about lube? Is it that Vald is capable of natural lubrication? We can certainly say that Halvir used magic, and since this BL is a fantasy one, well, we could go there. However, if you were to write a soft novel out of this, it would feel very unnatural. While it's true that explaining all the preparation would be boring, you can certainly add something and make it fun without dwelling on it too much.

COOL TROPES

There're some tropes that are cool and that mixing them, matching them and playing with them seems like a good idea. Not all tropes are bad, but they can be if used badly. So, as with all things: be careful. The best thing to do is to read a lot in the genre you want to write and take a moment to see how the author used the tropes. (Also, not everything that is in the mainstream is good. Be aware of that too when you buy romance from main publishers).

Most common romance tropes

- Love at first sight
- Secret billionaire
- From enemies to lovers
- From friends, to enemies, to lovers
- Arrogant playboy finally finds his heart
- Forced proximity (unwilling roommates, unwilling coworkers, etc)
- Hey! There's only one bed in this room!
- Boy next door
- Forbidden love
- Second chance romance
- Soul mates

Don't be afraid of tropes

In short: don't be afraid of tropes. True, there're some that are poisonous and should be eradicated from the literary world. But some others are nice. Many tropes have been super-used but that doesn't mean that you cannot use them at all. The challenge is to use them in a different way, half making your readers expect one thing and then surprising them with something better. So, aim for that!

EIGHT
THE ROLE OF AUTHOR'S NOTES IN FAN-FICTION

You can find "author notes" at the beginning of fan fiction stories at forums. Although each forum sight might have different rules, the idea of the "author's notes" it's to give a glimpse to your readers in case they should encounter any triggers in your story. Some authors choose not to give any warnings, and some give partial warnings. It's actually up to you; however, I consider it a very good idea to have some "author notes" at the beginning of your story.

Now, a very important thing to remember is that "author notes" are not there to spoil you story. Don't write too many information there! Just hints of some triggers, not spoilers off your work!

Books usually don't have these type of warnings because they are "kind of" included in the description of the book. However, it would be nice if you would warn somehow at the beginning of the book of warnings that might trigger some readers. It will be seen as a courtesy and you might avoid bad reviews on the Kindle Store.

WHERE TO PLACE THE AUTHOR'S NOTES

To make things easy, you should place your author's notes at the beginning, basically before starting the story. Refrain from placing them in the middle of the story because it disrupts it and then they don't make sense at all either. Warnings should be placed at the beginning, not in the middle and not at the end of the story.

Write them sweet and short. Don't spoil your story and don't write too many explanations. People will either skip reading those or skipping your story entirely!

Finally, try to refrain from irony since in the warnings. These should be informative, not a joke. Their aim is to warn readers of something that might trigger them.

———

THE BIG WARNINGS

I call big warnings the ones that are very important, including some general ones. These should tell you, at least roughly, what you should encounter while reading your book.

Choose not to use warnings

I know, it sounds weird, but choosing to write author's notes with a phrase that states "choose not to use warnings" is actually a warning in fan fiction forums. And, as a matter of fact, should be stated in the author's notes in most online forums. So, if you choose to surprise your reader (at their own peril), please state that you chose not to disclose anything.

In books this wouldn't be necessary since books are usually published without warnings and relying on people reading the book descriptions.

No warnings apply

If you story does not contain any violent depictions, nor any major character deaths, no rape, no underage sexual activity, and nothing of that sort, then state that "no warnings apply".

———

AGE RATINGS IN FAN FICTION

K: content suitable for most ages, above 5 or older. This is for stories that have no foul language, violence, and/or adult themes. This is the equivalent in shows of the G rating.

K+: it means that there's some content that's suitable for children below the age of around 9 years old. There might be some violence without serious injuries and there might be some foul language justified by the context and plot. This is the equivalent of a PG rating in movies.

T: it is not suitable for children but yes for teens. So, it would not be suitable for those younger than 13 years old. It might contain some violence, suggestive material, even drug abuse, but all are justified. This is the equivalent of PG-13 in movie ratings.

M: it's okay for mature teens and older folk. So it's for 16 year-old teens and older. It may contain non-explicit adult themes, violence (including sexual) and swearing and even drug abuse. This would be the equivalent of an R rating in movies.

MA: it means that it's only for a mature audience only and it might contain foul language and adult themes. This would be the equivalent of an NC-17.

AGE RATINGS IN THE PUBLISHING WORLD

Age ratings in the publishing world come from the genre the book belongs to. If you're writing young adult stories, then your book is targeting a teen audience. However, if your story is a new adult one, then your book is targeting people that range 18 to 25 years old.

Hence, there's no need to rate your story since the genre umbrella you'll place it will already be the rating itself.

MORE WARNINGS

GRAPHIC DEPICTIONS OF VIOLENCE

If there's any graphic depiction of violence in your story, you should state it in your author's notes. Now, just state the phrase but do not explain what's about. Remember: don't spoil your novel.

MAJOR CHARACTER DEATH

To be honest, I hate when major characters die, specially if it's my favorite. I do appreciate when I find a huge warning in the author's notes that will prepare me for doomsday. Again: do not spoil your story!

RAPE/ NON-CON (NON-CONSENSUAL)

If there's rape or non-consensual relationships in your story: please by all means, write it on your author's notes. I personally do mind about this topic, and I'm pretty sure many other people do get nervous with it. I like to be aware of what I'm going to encounter. Also, some people do get heavily triggered by it, so please remember to write a note about it. I know I'm a pain in the ass: please don't spoil your story. Basically, just write something like "warning: rape" and nothing else.

Please be mindful of this topic and use it appropriately or it can backfire easily.

UNDERAGE

The same as with rape/non-con, remember to state if there're triggering underage topics. In the same fashion as above, some of your readers might get triggered by it. Obviously, if your main character is a 2,000-year-old vampire trapped in a 16-year-old body, then please be consistent. Meaning, the character will still be an adult. Even if you use your better judgement, I'd recommend to write the warnings anyway. Again: please don't spoil your story. (As you might have noticed: I'm not a huge fan of spoilers).

This is also a very thorny topic and should be use with care and in drama stories. You might be caving your own grave in the publishing arena if you start being insensitive with your readers and falling into nasty tropes.

FANDOMS

If you're writing a story inspired to some fandom, please state that in your author's notes. While in forums you can get away with sharing fandom fan fiction, in the publishing arena you'd be breaking some copyright rules! Hence, it's paramount to be aware that what you can share in a forum might not be adapt to be published and monetized.

You can certainly be inspired by books and write your own take, like *The Court of Thorns and Roses* (a new take on the Beauty and the Beast).

Relationships in fan fiction

Think about categories as hashtags on Instagram. Most of these are related to the types of pairings that you might encounter during the story. Some are pretty straightforward.

- **F/F**: Female x female.
- **F/M**: Female x male.
- **M/M**: Male x male.
- **Multi**: There's a relationship with multiple partners.
- **Other**: Any other thing that might come to mind. For example, aliens and you don't want to classify them.
- **About the pairings**: When you write about fandom pairings, use a slash. Very much like in slash fiction. For example, Spock/Kirk or Thor/Loki. You can also try with combinations of names, for example Thorki. But in the case you made up the name, I'd also write the full name in this fashion: Thorki (Thor/Loki).
- **Canon / non-canon (canonical / non-canonical)**: Canon just means canonical. If you write a fan fiction piece according to the main story, or canon, then you

would write "canon" in your author's notes. And if it doesn't, please write "non-canon".

While these are very welcomed in fan fiction forums, there's no need to add them at the beginning of your book. You can create your own unique pairing names so that readers can later on create fan fiction stories of your original characters, or even share a special chapter with all the juicy information or writing prompts that you could gift your readers should they want to imagine alternate universes with your original characters.

CO-AUTHORSHIP

If you write your story alongside with friends, all of you are co-authors. In this case, please always name them in the author's note in the fan fiction forum. In the same fashion, if you self-publish the story as a book, please remember to name everyone involved in writing the story or illustrating it (that includes the cover of the book!)

THAT THING CALLED COPYRIGHT

An important thing to take into consideration is copyright. It involves the authors that wrote the story, but also if you based your story in another exiting one (for example: Thorki). In that case, you're writing fan fiction and the fair use clause allows you to do so. However, you cannot monetize that story.

You need to write original characters and original stories in order to self-publish your book.

OTHER INFORMATION TO CONSIDER

ADAPTATION

If it's an adaptation of an existing story, please also state that.

Alternate Universe

It's when you take the characters of an existing story and put them in a different setting. This is completely different from a divergence, since you put your characters in a different setting. (It's not a "what if?")

Again, if you're using already existing and copyrighted characters, you're writing fan fiction and cannot be monetized.

Continuation

If you like a story and want to continue it after it ends, then you're on the works of a continuation. It's a hard thing to do because if it's well written, it means that you're following the same style, and the character's fashion.

As with the category above, you cannot monetize your story if you're using already existing characters that you didn't imagine at all.

Divergence

This is when you take an already existing story at a certain point and ask yourself "what if?" And you answer it by writing a story. As fan fiction this can help you flex the writing muscle. But remember that this would be fan fiction and cannot be monetized either.

Elsewhere Fic

When you take the setting but forget the characters to write your story. A good example of this would be using Dungeons and Dragons setting and you create brand new characters to play. (You get what I mean).

- **OC**: Original character.
- **OFM**: Original female character.
- **OMC**: Original male character.

———

Remember that if you're used to write fan fiction, you can't just format it into a Kindle Book and make all the cash from it. Copyright rules are very serious. Nobody says you can't get inspired by a story, but this is all about you can do: get inspired. You need to write your own stories and then you can monetize them by self-publishing.

NINE
FAN-FICTION AND COPYRIGHT

So, we hit the very hot potato: fan fiction and copyright. From all the spicy topics, I consider copyright the beast. Nope, it wasn't sex, mind you, but copyright. From all the headaches you can ever get, copyright it's the biggest. Why? Because there's a very fine line to walk when you're writing fan fiction of already existing characters as they are. So, yeah, Thorki? IronFrost? Yup, all that super-mega-copyrighted by the big Disney.

So, what to do if you want to write a fan fiction from existing characters that you'd like to later self-publish?

Good question.

Very good one, especially if you're super proud of what you've written so far.

THE TWO BIG "BOO-BOOS"

You can't just use someone else's characters to your new story and then self-publish your brand new book. What you can do is to "base something on" or create a "retelling" with original characters. Huge books out there are based in other stories, like Sarah J. Maas' A Court of Thorns and Roses, aka ACOTAR.

Also, you cannot rip off a story just by writing something and then changing the names of the characters and places. Even if you take those from an unknown forum lost in the Bahamas of internet: you can't do that.

The only thing you can self-publish are "original stories" or stories who got inspiration in other stories but are totally different. (Please refer to ACOTAR as an example).

BIG BOO BOO NUMBER 1: USING THE CHARACTERS AS THEY ARE

You can just take the characters of a story, write your take and self-publish it. The copyright monsters will take you away, tuck you in a bed of thorns and forget you while you scream in agony.

Legit story.

BIG BOO BOO NUMBER 2: YOU CANNOT RIP OFF ANYONE ELSE'S WORK!

You can't use someone else's work as your own. Period. It doesn't matter if they're a big guy or a small guy. It doesn't matter if you found that in an unknown blog. You can get "inspo" from it, but you can't simply take it and that's it.

FAIR USE

According to the Wikipedia, fair use is "one of the limitations to copyright intended to balance the interests of copyright holders with the public interest in the wider distribution and use of creative works by allowing as a defense to copyright infringement claims certain limited uses that might otherwise be considered infringement."

So, what does that mean? In simple words, it means that you can write parodies, write research works, and report on them. As long as it falls in one of the categories of "fair use" you'll be safe. So, what if your work does neither of those? What if it's just hot entertainment? Well, then you'll have to prove it's fair use. Unless you're making profit out of it (like in money) odds are that if your story is not damaging, not lucrative and you're sharing it just because of sharing it you'd be fine.

That being said, because it's a very fine line we're walking when writing fan fiction (wink wink to Marvel), if the behemoth copyright holder comes and knocks on your door, you'll need to take it down.

Now, how far can we argue that BL is for "educational purposes"?

Not sure? Please read the wikipedia for legal issues with fan fiction: https://en.m.wikipedia.org/wiki/Legal_issues_with_fan_fiction

PART TWO
WRITING BL ROMANCE

TEN
TYPES OF BL CHARACTERS

Traditionally, in BL you have different types of characters. However, you don't need to use the traditional "cookie-cut" characters described below. I would recommend that you treat your characters by their personality traits mainly as to make them as human as possible.

To make the pair of lovers work, you should make their personalities sparkle or be contradictory somehow (more on that in the next chapter).

Broadly speaking there are three main types of BL characters: the dominant, the submissive, and the switch. And yes, it does sound a lot like entering the arena of BDSM.

LET'S MEET OUR HEROES

You'll notice a lots of tropes below with the descriptions of the traditional types of *yaoi* characters. The thing to shine is to make bold and amazing characters, and hence, you can totally smash the tropes!

Seme 「攻め」

The seme is the dominant one in a BL couple. It's a quite graphic way to point at the dominant homosexual partner since the verb *semeru* means to attack. However, this is one of the many words that we can use for the dominant guy. Others include "Tachi" 「タチ」 and *hidarigawa* 「左側」 (literally, "left side.")

To call someone *seme* is just using a general term. Some characters have others quirks. In that case, we can find words like *souseme* 「総攻め」 perfect dominant, *tachisen* 「タチ専」 or complete dominant (as a fetish, basically), and *dakisen* 「抱き専」 or clingy seme (he likes to embrace a lot.) But wait, there're more sub-types of *seme*!

Super Seme-Sama: 「スーパー攻め様」 is the quintessential type of *seme*. He's stylish, good-looking, confident, and super manly. But it's also serious and wants to do his way all the time, even if it means doing it by force. (*Super Seme-Sama* example: Asami from the Finder series by Ayane Yamano)

Kotoba Seme: 「言葉攻め」 is a dominant guy that likes to play with words while doing it with his partner. He usually whispers all types of obscene words and insults to make him hotter than he is at the moment.

Keigo Seme: 「敬語攻め」 is a dominant guy that likes to be super polite while doing it and uses honorific words while they're making love. This would work perfectly in Japanese because the honorific register of the language allows for it. In English might not work as perfectly and it can result in a very weird way where the dominant partner talks too politely!

Ayamari Seme: 「謝り攻め」 is a *seme* that uses excuses and apologies while they're at it. It can be that the *seme* knows that he's doing the wrong thing and he's apologizing while he's forcing his partner. (This one is not cool at all!)

Uke 「受け」

The *Uke* is the submissive partner in a homosexual relationship. The word is also pretty descriptive since it comes from the verb *ukeru* or to receive. There are other words to call the *uke*, for example, *neko* 「ネコ」 cat, and *migigawa* 「右側」 which literally means "right side."

When the guy is always an *uke* regardless of the partner, we're talking about a perfect *uke*, or *sou-uke* 「総受け」. But, as happens with the *seme*, there're many other sub-types of *ukes*. (*Sou-uke* example: Akihito from the Finder series by Ayane Yamano)

Inran Uke:「淫乱受け」 is an *uke* who is eager to do it at any time. He's lascivious, wild, and lewd. It can also be that the *uke* is profoundly affected by the sexual relationship with his current partner.

Joou-sama Uke:「女王様受け」 means "princess uke". This type of *uke* is mean. They're beautiful, but they show off in a pompous manner because they know they're like queens for the *seme*. They have power or authority over the *seme*. And they can be oppressive and extremely mean. But, the *seme* are so in love that they let them do whatever they want.

Bitch:「ビッチ」 is an *uke* that has a very disordered sex life or one that has many partners. Or it could be a very sad *uke* that ends up having lots of sex just because he feels very lonely. Please note the word is only used with *ukes*. And yes, it can come as very deprecating since there's an equivalent with women. Welcome to the trope world of BL manga.

Seke「セケ」

A *seke* (or switch) is someone who will be a *seme* or an *uke* depending on the partner, or even with the current partner. They like to do everything.

———

Now that we have the type of characters, we need to take a look at the words referring to the couples. In *yaoi*, there're different types of couples. However, the main word to say couple in Japanese is just "coupling."

(See - switch- example: *Yuri Ayato from Yarichin Bitch Club by Ogeretsu Tanaka*)

Coupling「カップリング」

Aka shipping or pairing. This word can be shortened as only CP, or *kapu*. However, couples or ships are best known for saying the names of the characters using an x in the middle. For example,

Thor x Loki. But, you can shorten that by using a combination of the names. In this case, we'd call this ship Thorki. It's pretty straightforward, isn't it?

You can create the own names of the couple in the book and help readers talk about the pairing.

Sub-Cup 「サブカプ」

Aka sub-couple is the short for a secondary ship that might appear in the BL manga. While some fans can go crazy with the first couple, others might swoon for the sub-couple.

Riba 「リバ」

Riba is the short version of "reversible couple." It's a ship where both *uke* and *seme* exchange roles in their relationship. This is quite an egalitarian coupling.

Yuripple 「百合ッブル」

A *yuripple* is a ship where there are two *ukes*. Both love one another, and both are *ukes*. "Yuri" comes from the Girls Love arena, where *yuri* means "lily."

Seme-seme/ kou-kou 「攻x攻」

A *kou-kou* is a ship where two *semes* love each other. They might even take turns to be the *uke*, but they are in endless competition. Because they're rivals and they love each other, the problems in the coupling are secured. Hence, the appeal for this type of coupling.

WAYS TO CALL EACH OTHER

We're going to also take a look at what the lovebirds might call each other. Although each manga will show different ways, there is a general convention on how *semes* and *ukes* might call each other.

Muko 「婿」

Muko means husband or groom. So, if an *uke* calls "my husband" to his partner, he's affectionate. It can also be that fans use the word *muko* to point out who the dominant partner might be in the ship without using the words *seme* or *tachi*.

Yome 「嫁」

Yome means wife or bride. If a *seme* calls "my wife" to his *uke*, then he's affectionate (or ironic, depending on the manga). It can also be that the fans are using *yome* to point out who the passive partner might be in a coupling without using the words *uke* or *neko*.

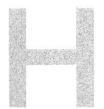

———

HONORABLE MENTIONS

Age gap coupling: when the age gap between the seme and uke is substantial.

Bishonen: aka "bishies," are very good-looking men.

Crack Ship/Pairing: is a type of extreme shipping. It happens when fans ship impossible couples, that most probably kill each other than make sex together. It can also be that the ship is so far away from the official canon that it's impossible to come true. You have to be on "crack" to believe that it would either happen or that the characters wouldn't kill each other.

Kagema: are male prostitutes that usually take the role of an *uke*. You might find this word mostly in historical *yaoi*. (I wouldn't write a historical setup without proper research, specially if you set it in Japan).

Rotten talk: is the conversations that *fujoshi/fudanshi* have when talking about BL. It can be as naive as just naming the ship they like, or as hot as *heavy-fangirling* on a BL manga.

Slash: is shipping characters of the same sex in fan fiction. This word can be used as a way to explain BL, and even as an equivalent. But it's mainly used in the realm of fan fiction.

Younger Seme: when the dominant in the couple is younger than the submissive partner.

ELEVEN
CHOOSE YOUR LEAD CHARACTERS

Any type of romance requires a strong character growth, hence choosing your lead characters is the most important part of the story. If they don't connect with your readership, your story is… well… doomed. In short: romance is highly character-driven and not as much story-driven.

The two love interests need to have some sort of conflicting traits to create personal conflict and drive the romance forward along with something that the characters learn from each other. The more tension you create, the more likely your readers will be hooked with your story.

TYPICAL CONFLICTING PAIRINGS

- Arrogant vs low self-esteem
- Timid vs brazen
- Introverted vs extroverted
- Grumpy cat vs sunshine and rainbows.

You get the picture? Think about Ten Count. What are Shirotani's and Kurose's traits? What interpersonal conflicts arise from these and how the romance is driven by the author along the series?

CHOOSE YOUR LEAD CHARACTERS   47

Let's think about the following (it'll help you in creating these antagonistic traits in your characters):

- How are your characters going to grow emotionally and personally together?
- How is their love changing them for the better?
- What flows do they overcome by learning from each other?

MAKE YOUR CHARACTERS FIT THE SUB-GENRE YOU CHOSE!

It might seem obvious but, if you're writing a contemporary romance, please don't put inside a vampire that has nothing to do with the setting. You still need to make the story believable for the reader while being also consistent with the market. Don't just write a story and put a werewolf in there so that you can place your novel in the paranormal shelf on the Kindle Store.

MAIN SEVEN CHARACTERS IN STORIES

You can make categories of characters depending on the role they play in your book. The easy examples are the main characters an the antagonist, aka the foe. But there're more than that:

- PROTAGONIST: this is the main character of the story. It can be just one person, or it can be more than one. They should be careful crafted and feel like a real person. For example, Bilbo, from the Hobbit, feels like the neighbor next door that doesn't look like it but they will succeed.
- ANTAGONIST (aka the FOE): this is the villain in the story, like Lex Luthor, the antagonist of Superman; Voldemort for Harry Potter; Miranda in the Devil Wears Prada. (You get the idea!) You can also have "anti-heroes" who have

a dual face living between the hero and the villain. Examples are Loki and the Punisher from the Marvel Universe.
- HANDSOME (aka the LOVE INTEREST): this is the love interest of the protagonist. They love them and yet they cannot get close to them just yet. Let's say "things are difficult".
- CONFIDANT (aka the BEST FRIEND): this is also seen as the sidekick (or Robin for Batman). The protagonist might need someone to talk to, someone who will always have their backs. This is it. For example, Hermione for Harry Potter.
- DEUTERAGONISTS (aka the OTHER BEST PAL): these are characters who overlap with the best friends but are not quite so. They're pretty close to the protagonist and help them somehow. For example, that would be Sam for Frodo in The Lord of The Rings; or Luna Lovegood for Harry Potter. (I know, wild!)
- TERTIARY CHARACTERS: these are the "secondary characters" who are there in the world in the story, but they might not even link to the main plot at all. These are minor characters that are very dynamic and they enhance the story somehow. For example, Parvati Patil in Harry Potter.
- FOILS: these are characters that bring the protagonist's abilities at the forefront. For example, think about Captain Kirk and Spoke. Without Spoke, Kirk is a little bit gray, isn't he?

You also have another way to see characters. Some are more dynamic than others, while some are super static. All of them serve some purpose within the story. For example:

- DYNAMIC CHARACTERS: dynamic characters are those who change with the unfolding events in the story. The

best dynamic character of all should be the protagonist since they cannot be the same again from the start to the end of the story.
- ROUND CHARACTERS: these characters are very similar to the dynamic ones and are also very fluid and changeable. However, they don't change until something happens. For example, Katniss won't change until her sister is in jeopardy.
- STATIC CHARACTERS: these characters don't change much during the course of the story. They might be somewhat flat, and usually play tertiary roles. Villains usually end up in that category (say hello to Voldemort!), but it shouldn't be that way.
- STOCK CHARACTER: these are archetypal characters with fixed personality traits. They won't change at all, and are there for a specific reason.
- SYMBOLIC CHARACTER: these are characters that represent a concept. Most of these are supporting characters, but in literature we do have protagonists! You can find one in The Idiot, from Dostoevsky.

―――――

CHARACTER ARCHETYPES

You might also find archetypical characters in literature. If you like Tarot like I do, then you might know Karl Jung. He was the master of archetypes (which, by the way, can be all found in the Major Arcana of the Tarot). According to him, there're 12 archetypes:

- THE HERO: this is the protagonist who rises to meet all challenges and save the day. They tend to be courageous, perseverant and honorable. However, they do have weaknesses. For example, being overconfident! Need some examples? Think about Luke Skywalker.

- THE LOVER: this is the romantic lead who is only lead by the heart and feelings. They're humanitarian and compassionate. On the flip side, they tend to be naive and maybe also irrational. Need an example? Think about Romeo.
- THE SAGE: this is a wise figure who will guide you in the dark times. They're wise beyond measure, experienced and also mysterious. On the flip side, they might be too curious. Need an example? Think about Gandalf.
- THE OUTLAW: this is a rebel who doesn't follow the rules. They could be the bad guy, but not always. (Loki or Han Solo, anyone?) They are smart, intelligent and sometimes even skeptical.
- THE MAGICIAN: they're powerful wizards who know the laws of the Universe. They're wise beyond measure and know when to act and when it's best to be dormant. However, they can also be corrupt. Famous Magicians are Gandalf, Dumbledore and in sci-fi, Morpheus.
- THE EXPLORER: this is a character driven by curiosity eager to test boundaries. Their main motivation is self-improvement. However, they can come up as somewhat unreliable and people who are hard to satisfy. The most famous example I can give you is Odysseus.
- THE INNOCENT: this is a naive character who might be a child or someone childish. Their intentions are good and are very kind and even fluffy. However, on the flip side, they're a liability.
- THE SAGE: this is a wise figure who knows everything either by experience or because of insight. They're too cautious and might be hard to move. You have a good example in Obi-Wan Kenobi.
- THE CREATOR: this is the motivated visionary that sees the future or creates fantastic machines or art. They're self-involved and somewhat single-minded.
- THE RULER: this is a very "legal" character that has

power over all the others. They might be omnipotent, have high-status and have all the resources of the land. However, they might come up as aloof and hated by others. A good example would be King Lear.
- THE JESTER: this is a funny character that gives comic relief but at the same time is able to speak the truth. They might also be super obnoxious.
- THE CAREGIVER: this is a character that always supports all the other characters and sacrifices for them whatever happens. They're honorable and selfless. But they can also have issues of self-steam.
- THE EVERYMAN: this is a character everyone can relate to and feel warm. They're grounded and very relatable. However, they don't have any special skills and are usually super underprepared for any adventure. A good example of this, believe it or not, is Bilbo from The Hobbit.

TWELVE
CREATE YOUR MAIN CHARACTER'S PROFILE

Although this chapter is called "create your character's file", in fact what we're going to talk about is "people". Say what? Yeah! We're going to talk about how to create people, not characters. According to Ernest Hemingway (shit, we're getting deep here):

> "when writing a novel a writer should create living people; people not characters. A character is a caricature".

So, why did I write that title? Because people are used to talk about characters in story-writing. Our target is to make our story compelling and our "characters" so real that they are people to whoever picks up our story and reads it.

CREATING PEOPLE, NOT CHARACTERS

We should have a very rough idea about our story, the baby steps of our plot. But for it to be brilliant, we need badass main characters that will steal your readers' hearts. So, we'll turn the idea of a character that you have in your mind into a full well-shaped person.

THE THREE MUSTS OF YOUR CHARACTER

CREATE YOUR MAIN CHARACTER'S PROFILE

All main characters need three fundamental things to make them compelling.

1. What does your character want from the real world? (A new house? A new job? Being rich?)
2. What does your character want emotionally? (Being loved? Feeling fulfilled as an artist?)
3. This one is f***g crucial: why can't they have these? (Do they have a shitty job and no saved money for the house? Are they engulfed in loans and homeless? Were they mistreated by their previous partner and now they're afraid of trying again with love?)

This is where we start the hole thing! It might seem simple, but when we'll expand this is might get tricky.

Let's get an example with "Ten count" from Rihito Takarai. Misotani wants to be loved but he has *mysophobia*, a fear of germs. He wears gloves, washes his hands constantly, and has his house pristine. He is a valuable asset at his job, and yet he is miserable! (See where I'm going here?)

Misotahi is "self-sabotaging" himself (no friends, no real life to be honest) because he suffers from *mysophobia*. This phobia will bring him to therapy, and then eventually love. But until he can arrive to his happy ever after, he has to suffer the troubles and misfortunes that Rihito sets for him to cure him so that they can be together.

Misotani can have love because he's scared shitless that something will happen to him if he's polluted. Because, the world is a scary, very scary place!

ADDING DEPTH TO YOUR VICTIMS… AHEM, I MEAN, CHARACTERS

The thing that is preventing your character of having what they want is what you think you'll need to solve for them to be happy. In other to add depth to your characters, you'll need to… drumroll…

create more problems for them! Yeah, I know, writers are utter bastards. (Hush, hush, you're one of them.)

Think about your own life. Do you just need to deal with one problem, really? Nope. You usually focus on one thing, but there's more things out there bugging you. These extra problems are the different arcs in your story. (Wink, wink, this is a glorious way to get readers hooked!)

Your main characters have to be as complex as you are! Think about Misotani. Is his mysophobia the only thing affecting him? There're many other things attached: he feels not enough, he's too shy when interacting with other people, and he feels so withdrawn from the world that it's obvious that he's utterly afraid to even try by himself. (And yet, we know what happens next to him. And that's why we're so hooked with his story!)

So, you do have your gorgeous hero, right? And by now we do know what they want (in the world and emotionally) and why they cannot have it. Now, add (arbitrary number here) another six shitty problems into their lives! Yup, that's it! Add another six problems! (I know, so far, we're just throwing a bunch of shit to our main characters).

So, let's imagine this:

1. The physical problem: mysophobia.
2. The emotional problem: I'm not good enough to be love, I'm rubbish.
3. The social problem: all those germs everywhere, how can I ever attend that party?
4. The belief problem: I will never be accepted because I'm dirty as fuck. Only when I get super clean I'll be happy.
5. The real problem: being afraid of failure. What happens if I mess up? I have to face reality once I stop washing up my hands really. I'm just... normal?
6. The lifestyle problem: now I can control everything! The dust is gone in my apartment. I control utterly everything, only that reality is that nothing can be controlled and I fell

uneasy thinking that I can't control life! And all those horrible things that happened to me? It wasn't my fault but I want to think they were.

So, now you have Misotani as an example. Think about Harry Potter now. (I know, we go from romance to kids' fantasy, but hey, this is an exercise.) You can see the whole issue of what he wants, why he cannot get it. We can also see how others think he's super, but in reality he's just a normal kid.

1. The family problem: he's an orphan and he misses his parents, plus he lives with a family that really don't love him at all and make him live under the stairs!
2. The emotional problem: he believes that he's not good enough. Bullied and being an outsider all the time, he doesn't easily find his place in the world.
3. The social problem: he's a second-class member in his family and mistreated all the time. Because of this, when he discovers that he's a wizard that *will safe the world of "you know who"* he cannot really believe in himself.
4. The belief problem: he feels not enough and more muggle than a wizard. Plus, the new bullies appearing in his life only reaffirm this.
5. The real problem: he needs to learn how to stand for himself without leaning into the revenge arena just because he's been deeply emotionally wounded.
6. The lifestyle problem: he has no money, he's an orphan, and even if he has help, he just feels as an outsider.

Take your main character and just got through the *shit* we described above. So, do you have all the problems you need to start having your character being human?

The looks

Now we have to think about the looks of your character. While readers don't want to read 10 pages on how your character looks, we can have a pretty good picture as the story evolves. Unless you're describing a hot scene in your story, I'd refrain to giving too many details on your character's looks. Seriously, leave something to the imagination of your readers!

Showing is more effective than telling. "Show, don't tell" is a writing technique where you illustrate instead of just telling what's going on.

- Showing: "he found himself in the corner of the room squeezing the pillow in all the directions his hands allowed him. He held his breath while staring at the furry tiny mouse while sweating and trying to decide if jumping quickly on the creature towards the door would save his life.
- Telling: Olly was terrified by the little mouse in his room.

Instead of just saying that Olly is afraid of mice, showing how he reacts to a little mouse in his room is far more effective and is more fun, don't you think?

What your character does speaks volumes

We judge people by their actions, what they wear (yup, fashion), if they have tattoos or not. Basically, describing roughly a character and telling what they do in detail is more powerful than giving me an exhaustive description on their looks. The same happens with steamy scenes: do you really want to know how blond the beard was? Or are you more interested on what's going on and what the kiss made your main character feel?

Basically: it's how your characters react to situations that will speak volumes about your characters, more than super gritty-bitty descriptions of their muscles.

So, now that we're here, let's brainstorm and write about your main characters.

1. Someone provokes them. How do they react? (Think

about situation where you're bullied by someone, for example).
2. Now, you have a memory pop up in your characters head and they're triggered. How are they reacting to that memory?
3. How other people react to their quirks?
4. How they react to other people?
5. How does your character with their environment?

THE BACKSTORY

Okay, now you have the best idea of your character. You also know how to make their life impossible. Now, how did they arrive to that point? All characters need a backstory we can go back at any point. You don't need to write a whole book about their story, you just need to have an idea and some lines of what happened to their lives to be who they are.

Think about how your memory works. You do not remember absolutely everything that happened into your life really. You just remember some stuff, and those highlights are enough as to explain to someone about your life. Think about the time you made your first kiss. Do you actually remember every single detail of the place you were? All the conversation you had before that? All the food and how it tasted before the deed happened?

All these highlights will make your character a person. So, it's your job to have enough highlights as to make your character human. You see? You don't need to have all the details, just some highlights of key moments in their lives to make them who they're when the reader meets them in your story.

Now, think about 10 memorable events of your character's life and write them down. This will help you to have a complex character and also to add some of these events into the *sh***t* you make them go through! (I know, we're evil. Please drop the mike along with me).

THIRTEEN
SPICE UP YOUR CHARACTERS

I just put a nice pic here as a distraction. The same goes for the title: spicing up your characters. It's a trap. I just wanted to say that this whole section should have been titled:
HOW TO BE A BLOODY BASTARD TO YOUR CHARACTERS

I know, that's evil. But the worse you get, the better it will be. How so? Would you keep reading a story where there's no tension? Where characters are perfect? Where everything is given without any troubles? No, I wouldn't. I would be so boring!

But what if you almost can touch it but then it's fucked up and then you have to fix things and then you make them worse and then it looks like you get it and then you fuck it even worse than before? Oh, yeah, I'm all for it! Because, when the end of the book comes and if they do get it (or not, if you want a tragic story) it's going to be so epic you wish your favorite book will never end. Please, favorite writer, keep being an utter bastard to your characters!

And yup, that's how it works! (Now, if your plan was world domination and being an utter bastard, this is for you!)

THE THING YOUR CHARACTER WANTS AND WHY THEY CAN'T HAVE IT

It's all about that. It starts wanting something and you not giving it to them! That's the big picture, what the whole story is all about.

And with BL, it's about love. It can be either that they want love and they cannot get it because of something (Ten Count), or that they want someone in particular and someone else is in the way (love triangles! Yes please!)

But, do I need to stop here being an utter bastard to my characters? Is one problem ever enough?

INCREMENTAL LEVELS OF *DOUCHERY*

Screw your main characters in incremental steps. (And by the end of the run, give them what hey want because this is BL and we all want that steamy scene! But before that: make them suffer!)

I know: basically what I'm saying is to be an utter bastard to your character because you're going to make your readers invested in the story and you're going to torture them emotionally wanting them to keep up reading until, after so much hurdles, the deed will be done!

I know... utter evil!

THE EVIL QUEENS EXERCISE OF MAKING YOUR CHARACTER'S LIFE IMPOSSIBLE

Now that we have internalized that we're utter bastards, we need to take our main character and think about incremental ways of fucking up their lives. (I don't write f***g much like this anymore because we have already stablished that we're utter evil. Ha!)

So, for example:

1 Let's say my main character, called Takui, wants to be a singer but he's utterly shy and has a huge phobia of talking in public. (Sing in public? Forget it!)

2 To make matters worse, when he gets nervous he stutters when he gets nervous.

3 Plus, the last time he was in a karaoke bar his best friend made fun of him and the whole bar laughed their asses off.

4 Plus, he likes a guy that looks like exactly the best friend that made fun of him, and though he likes him a lot, he also triggers all the bad memories and he also stutters when he tries to talk to him.

5 Plus, there's this contest going on in the karaoke in the music

genre he loves and he knows he's good at but cannot bring himself to even try…

6Plus, he's having all these wet dreams with the guy that looks like his torturer.

You get the picture.

SPICING THINGS UP AND MESSING YOUR CHARACTER'S PSYCHE… YEAH, EVEN FURTHER!

So, now that we've stablished that we're evil and that we're making our main character's life a friggin' hell, we need to mess up the steam romance. Yup. Don't give your audience what they want easily: make the pressure go up, up, and up. Give them the taste, just a bit, then make them droll.

I'm serious.

Create problems, make them seem like there's a fix working. Then make things worse with an utter crises, and then change something, and finally, give to your audience the steam that they deserve!

Ten Count

In Ten Count, Shitorani has a compulsive disorder and mysophobia. He needs to repeat certain actions and be super clean (and his surroundings too) to be happy. He meets Kurose and because he's a therapist he decides to get his help. But he also likes Kurose. His therapist asks him to list ten things he cannot do, and they'll go through these in order to cure him. (Big ahem, steam on, my friends!)

While Shirotani gets repulsed and happy with the advances of Kurose, the therapist ends up revealing himself as a sadist? (Wait what!???) Kurose loves triggering Shirotani's mysophobia? Wait, what!??? For real?? Obviously Shirotani goes into his turtle shell and stops talking to Kurose for months! Was he even getting cured at some point really? Was it all just a game?

They end up meeting again, and then they make up. Shirotani has grown and is comfy enough to confess that the tenth item in the list (that he left blank at the beginning) was something as simple as being accepted. Kurose had lied to Shirotani as well, and hold and behold, he actually asks Shirotani to create a list for things that he wants him to do. Now, they both are in the same page and exchange love in the same amounts.

But before we arrived there, we suffered for several volumes filled with tension and utter more tension of OMG-moments and distress!

Nothing has more tension than romance

Romance tension is the top of tensions in the literary world. Build tension up until your readers are desperately keeping reading to know if their favorite pairing will finally kiss or go beyond that kiss they had after taking a coffee together in a very questionable strip club. (You get the feeling).

Basically put, don't give your characters any easy any time soon because you don't want your readers to have it easily either.

BOUM.

I'm evil. Yes! So you should be too!

FOURTEEN
DO YOU NEED WORLD-BUILDING IF I'M WRITING ROMANCE?

Well, so do you really need world-building in romance, a genre that's basically character-driven? well, the answer is… drumroll!

You still need world-building because a good BL romance (not erotica, mind you) needs a story, especially if you're writing fantasy! The world the story takes place is important because it'll affect also how the characters will interact in society and with each other. The setting is paramount to understand also where they come from. For example, something as simple as: what are the social expectations for each of your characters? Do they have a very traditional family that want them married with kids?

So, we'll need:

- A good setting, so the readers know the starting point and will have a rough idea on what to expect.
- Social class, so we know a bit more about your characters. If one is a billionaire and the other is a waiter, they cannot have exactly the same hobbies, can they? They will also have different views on money, how much they can spend, or if they are more or less greedy. (You get the point).

- Belief system. If they come from a very traditional family and then they fall in love with someone considered as forbidden, their belief system is going to be challenge and one of the obstacles they'll need to overcome to be happy.
- Societal norms. If you write the setting in a timeframe where same-sex couples are banned or not well-perceived, this is going to deeply affect your characters too.
- Your character's jobs. As I mentioned above, if someone is a waiter and the other is a billionaire who has never worked before, that is going to color their views of the world, etc.

You don't need to be super-realistic. You just need to be consistent with your choices so it'll feel believable. You cannot write impediments in their love story as being forbidden love in an open-minded society.

FIFTEEN
CREATING A TIMELINE

So, why should we be creating a timeline? Well, to have an idea to where the story should go. Also, it will help us to know more about our characters and their circumstances. Let's say that the timeline goes in our present time, in Tokyo, such us in the way it does in Ten Count. That would be completely different if we had the set up in London, where there's wizards and an alternate Universe below what we can see. (Yup, I was talking about Harry Potter there). Also, it'll be completely different if we set up our story in the middle ages or in a fantasy world like the Witcher's.

Just having a timeline of sorts, even if we will change it later (and believe me, we will) it'll help us massively in setting up all full story and what the characters will do (or should be doing) at a certain point.

So, take a pen and a piece of paper and line up the major events of the timeline of the story that you want to tell. Yup, just the major events.

So, to have an idea. Let's take a look at (I know, has nothing to do with romance, but it'll work for you to get the taste) Erin Brockovich. (Now go and watch the movie before proceeding to read!)

1. The setup

We start Erin's story with her completely broke. She's an unemployed mom that cannot find a job. To make matters worse, she has been hit by a car and loses the lawsuit. So, bit meh.

The setting has to reveal what's going on in the life of your main character, and it has to be compelling for the readers to continue reading. The character has to connect with the reader somehow: sympathetically, emotionally, or because they might be likable or funny.

2. The opportunity

Erin ends up forcing Ed Masry to give her a job (she's desperate, duh!)

There has to be some sort of opportunity for your main character to do something, which will create the new journey for them. It doesn't need something major like forcing someone to give you a job; it could be something as simple as taking a coffee with their crush.

3. The new situation

Erin begins working in Ed's law firm and start learning more about lawsuits. She also meets her neighbor George who she fancies. Also, she starts investigating a case! And then… she gets fired.

Your main character now is in a new situation very different they have been before. So, how will they react? What's going to happen? (Be a bastard and fire them! We talked about that before, and as you can see with Erin, things went worse, ha!) So, now that they're in utter shit, they have to figure out what to do next to get what they want.

AND THEN… THERE'S "THE TURNING POINT"

Erin ends up being hired again because she's the only one that knows about that new case she was investigating on her own. (You didn't see that coming, did you!?)

So, now that you thought that everything is lost, there's a glimpse of light, a type of second opportunity where your main character can shine again. By now your audience should be rooting for your main character. Now they should want your main character to get what they want!

AN THEN... THERE'S "THE PROGRESS"

Erin gets some of the victims to hire Ed to represent them and she gets a boyfriend! Remember George? Yup, that one!

By now things should seem that are working for your main character. It looks like they're getting what they want and things are going smoothly.

AND THEN... THERE'S "THE POINT OF NO RETURN"

Erin and Ed file the lawsuit, but Ed's firm is small and the bad guys are huge. To make matters worse there's the threat that the judge might dismiss the case and there won't be any hope to settle the case.

So, once Erin and Ed have filed the case there's no way back! The same with your character: something must happen when the only option is to go forward!

This would be the middle of the story when your main character is committed to get what they want. They cannot go back by this point and they cannot be the same ever again.

4. And now things go to shit… again!

Erin is so busy that has a few time to see her boyfriend and her kids. Because Ed thinks he cannot handle such a case, he brings another bigger law firm which doesn't treat the plaintiffs as well.

The character has to have trouble in getting what they want. Their goal looks very far away and unachievable by now. Remember that we were bound to be very bad people? Yup, we're f***g up our main character big time! And the readers are loving it. They cannot stop reading by now!

AND THEN... THINGS GET EVEN WORSE!

Most of the plaintiffs are fed up and start withdrawing from the lawsuit. Plus George leaves Erin.

Okay, if you made things miserable for your character, now you have to make them worse. Your readers must think that everything is lost and your main character must put everything on the line. EVERYTHING.

5. The final push

Erin goes and rallies all families to agree for arbitration and find evidence of the evil firm that made them sick.

So, your character is beaten but not dead, so they must risk everything to make their last stand! By this point your audience has nibbled away their nails.

AND THEN... THERE'S "THE CLIMAX"

Erin and Ed win the settlement and George returns!

Here, the main character MUST face the biggest obstacle that prevents them to have what they want and overcome it somehow. (If your character is shy, and there's no other way to get their love, they end up kissing the person they love).

6. The aftermath

Erin gets a 2 million dollar bonus! She continues working for Ed, hey! *Niiiice!*

To make things click, you need to show up what happens next. Obviously, if you're planning to create a second part of the story (another book), then you need to start creating a new set up and leave your audience wanting more!

Most romance has a very nice aftermath, so you can indulge in unicorns.

SIXTEEN
STEPS THAT MUST APPEAR IN A BL (ROMANCE) NOVEL

In romance there're a set of steps that must appear for the readers to be hooked up. We're mostly used to get those hypes and lows from romance novels already. As readers, if we don't get them, we might feel bored and abandon the story for good.

If your aim is to release the story and ultimately get good writing stories and them self-publishing them on Amazon, then there's a set of basic rules that readers expect to find in romance.

1. Meet cute

So, he's a therapist who wants to help me and he looks just save enough (Shirotani meeting Kurose). Or accidentally takes pictures of a super badass and attractive Yakuza (Akihito meeting Asami).

Meeting the cute is the thing that will drive the story. And when they meet there has to be some type of sexy tension there, especially if they're very different from each other. Romantic tension plus a desire to know more is what will make your story jumpstart and your readers know what will happen next.

The meeting is the moment where we'll start discovering the dynamics of the pairing: how do they interact? Are they shy? Are they rude when talking? Remember: this will set up the tone for the whole story!

2. ROMANTIC TENSION AHOY!

We've seen this already, but I'll share this again:

Exactly what it looks like: super high level of romantic tension in there! There should be a minimum of three scenes where you can cut with a knife the sexual tension between the characters.

Think about what events will draw your characters together, and then make them suffer because they cannot have the other person just yet. (Yeah, authors are these cruel beings from hell. And we love them for that. Plus: you're becoming one of the tribe!)

Every time we have a highly romantic tension-filled scene, hint at any emotional baggage or obstacles that stops the characters to kiss each other madly so you build even more tension and you're by now invested to know how the hell they're going to overcome those obstacles to finally make-out! Also, hint at how loving each other might make your characters better and heal.

3. THE HAPPY COUPLE GETS TOGETHER AND THEN THE BASTARD OF THE AUTHOR COMES AND PUTS THEM APART... SAY WHAT?

Remember: we're here in in different levels of being bastards to our characters. So, if you make them kiss, then put them apart. You can't give a "happy-ever-after" just yet (that would be boring!)

So, think about ways to put them apart. For example:

Your couple finally made out and seem happy, but the next week the company one of them works for decides to send the guy away for a full year. (Say what!???)

They kiss but them something awful happens like: the ex appears out of nowhere and there's a misunderstanding, or they kidnap Akihito again! (You get the picture).

Their love is forbidden. Here comes the old-fashioned mom and discovers your couple and throws away one of them and all is a disaster: you must choose your family or him!

Okay, they're meeting in secret before they're discovered. Depending on the length on your story you can torture your readers wit this. (Ha! And you thought we weren't bastardizing enough!)

4. Happy for now…

If you're going to create a series like The Court of Thorn and Roses, you can't give a fixed "happily ever after". You just need to give a "happy for now" and leave the ending opened to more bastardy on our part as authors. So, what does a "happy for now" ending look for your characters?

So, your couple has overcome many obstacles now and they're happy. How does that look?

SEVENTEEN
THE HERO'S JOURNEY

Joseph Campbell wrote about explaining the "hero's journey" writing technique that's been out there for centuries. He outlines a narrative structure used from the adventures of Gilgamesh! This writing plot technique has 17 stages (you don't need to cover them all, but most of them) which can be gathered in these big moments:

1. The Departure

This is when Bilbo ends up joining the dwarfs in their adventure, the moment he sets his feet out from his comfortable home to never be the same hobbit ever again. (Damn Gandalf!)

This is the moment when the hero leaves the ordinary world and sets up for an adventure. It doesn't need to be action-packed, but there's an event that changes your character forever. They cannot be the same ever again after falling in love with their crush and kissing them!

2. The Initiation

This is the part where your main hero is going into adventuring and having many troubles and where everything seems lost. This is when they have to overcome all obstacles if they want to be happy again!

3. The Return

This is when Bilbo goes back home but things are different. He's happy again in his home, but the adventures he went through have changed him forever.

In your BL story, the love and adventures that the hero went through to be happy have made him a better person, changed him forever. (You get the picture, don't you?)

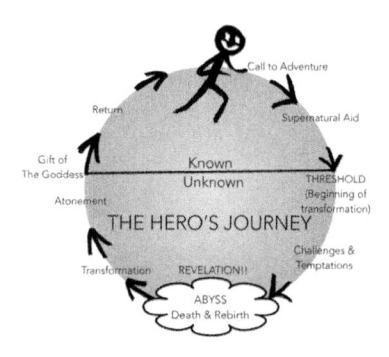

So, directly from the Wiki Page we get this:

Campbell (1949)

I. Departure

1. The Call to Adventure
2. Refusal of the Call
3. Supernatural Aid
4. The Crossing of the First Threshold
5. Belly of the Whale

II. Initiation

1. The Road of Trials
2. The Meeting with the Goddess
3. Woman as the Temptress
4. Atonement with the Father
5. Apotheosis

6. The Ultimate Boon

III. Return

1. Refusal of the Return
2. The Magic Flight
3. Rescue from Without
4. The Crossing of the Return Threshold
5. Master of the Two Worlds
6. Freedom to Live

David Adams Leeming (1981)

I. Departure

1. Miraculous conception and birth
2. Initiation of the hero-child
3. Withdrawal from family or community for meditation and preparation

II. Initiation

1. Trial and quest
2. Death
3. Descent into the underworld

III. Return

1. Resurrection and rebirth
2. Ascension, apotheosis, and atonement

Phil Cousineau(1990)

I. Departure

1. The call to adventure

II. Initiation

1. The road of trials
2. The vision quest
3. The meeting with the goddess
4. The boon

III. Return

1. The magic flight
2. The return threshold
3. The master of two worlds

Christopher Vogler(2007)

I. Departure

1. Ordinary world
2. Call to adventure
3. Refusal of the call
4. Meeting with the mentor
5. Crossing the first threshold

II. Initiation

1. Tests, allies, and enemies
2. Approach to the inmost cave
3. The ordeal
4. Reward

III. Return

1. The road back
2. The resurrection
3. Return with the elixir

Obviously, I'd choose the most recent version, but you get the picture of how this works. Basically, you make the life of your main character impossible, make them overcome obstacles, to finally grow as a person and be in the best situation possible to be happy with his loved one.

EIGHTEEN
BEGINNING, CLIMAX AND RESOLUTION

The beginning, climax and resolution structure is most commonly known as the "three act story structure". This one comes from screenwriting. This is the most commonly used writing plot structure ever.

So, it looks like this:

Act 1 - the setup

1. Inciting Incident
2. Plot point 1, that starts act 2

Act 2 - confrontation

1. Things happen
2. We arrive to the mid point
3. We get to the Plot point 2, that starts act 3

Act 3 - Resolution

1. Climax
2. The end (or plot point 4 that will start the second book!)

THE FIRST ACT

This is the opening of the narration and it usually establishes he main characters and their relationships while also setting up the world. After the description, there's either a happy accident ("meeting handsome") or a call to action (like Bilbo going on an adventure after being convinced by Gandalf and the dwarves in the movies). This catalyst will set up the story in motion whose life will never be the same again. Stakes rise as we proceed following the steps of the protagonist.

THE SECOND ACT

We find the protagonist trying to fix the mess created during the first act. They want to solve the problem, but they find themselves in even a bigger and growing mess (also known as "the author has been an utter bastard and is making my miserable life even worse!") Here we start to discover the skills of the protagonist and also we meet their antagonist who will confront them. So, the protagonist not only has to polish the skills they had, but also learn new ones, and save the day. All this character development is also known as the character's arc. They cannot achieve greatness without help. Hence, you'll need a nice bunch of co-protagonists too.

· · ·

THE THIRD ACT

Here we find the solution of the main plot and the solution of the subplots. The climax is the final scene where the hero wins and the villain is defeated. It's when we answer the big question posed during the first act when the protagonist "meets handsome". This doesn't need to be a "happy ever after" but it can also be a "happy for the time being", especially if you're thinking about writing a series.

Now take one of your favorite movies, one of your favorite books and one of your favorite comics and deconstruct them into the first, second, and third acts. What's the main plot? What are the subplots? How have these been answered at the end? It's any of those stories one in a series?

NINETEEN
BEING AN UTTER BASTARD TO YOUR CHARACTERS

This is my favorite one: levels of bastardy, or how awesome I am in creating problems for my characters. Yup, you guessed it! We have touched this topic with Erin's movie where she had more pain than gain, only to find her happy by the end of the movie (with boyfriend, a good job and a bonus of $2M!)

So, what's the "being a bastard technique"?

Well, it should look something like this:

The character is happy and meets cute.

Then the first problem happens: *mysophobia* (extreme or irrational fear of dirt or contamination)… damn!

I'm just going ahead and try to overcome that problem.

Damn! I made it even worse! (Now I'm pretty sure that I met a sadist! Never want to meet Kurose again!)

Seriously? Now someone else is making it worse too! (My life is miserable and I'm filth… serious filth… Shirotani goes on self-denial)

Wait, but I can fix it.

Nope, I can't, it's even worse and more complicated that before. (Why can't I stop thinking about Kurose!???)

Wait, the solution is there.

Wait again, nope it's my insecurity... oh no! Another problem? F***k!

And now there's a discovery! (Kurose lied and it's actually a super good guy)

Now everything seems okay, yay! But hey, leave it open for more problems to appear otherwise this will be the happy end of the story!

Hopefully, you got the picture of it. So, basically, you have to surprise the reader and make them wait for that happy ending and in the meanwhile be a machine of problems for your character. But you need to create problems that make sense within the story. Could you imagine a dinosaur appearing when Kurose and Shirotani are trying to have their first exchange? And suddenly they split because of a dino? It wouldn't make sense, would it?

IN SHORT, THIS IS WHAT SHOULD HAPPEN

1. THE BEGINNING

Your main character meets the cute guy and gets a crush on them. But they're shy, or there's some impediment. Regardless, they decide on going on this adventure called love.

2. THE MIDDLE

In the first half the main character is gathering skills while fucking up everything. Problems happen and everything seems lost but he's victorious. And then everything changes again! Damn!

And in the second half is when what else can go wrong? Seriously? Is there a god up there? (Yup, aka bastard writer who is making my life impossible staph it now!)

So there's a story arc: you start with something, you flip it, and then you turn it into something else so that your readers are now so invested in knowing what will happen with Shirotani that they can't wait for the next chapter. You simply can't stop reading!

3. THE END!

There's a happy ending but the characters have been changed forever. They're not the same: now they're better because of their love for each other.

CREATE CONFLICT

Let's be honest: without conflict and tribulations there wouldn't be any book worth reading. You need to raise the stakes as the story progresses, to make the tension stronger than ever, and to make the reader so invested that they would rob a bank for you in order for you to keep writing and being an utter bastard creating so many feelings for your favorite character.

Conflict is the gap between what your character wants and where they're now not having it! Make your character's life difficult, but also give some hope to your readers. Again: read Ten Count, it will help you getting an idea and lots of inspiration.

TWENTY
SEX AND STEAM

Now, time to steam things up! Those sexy scenes that readers are craving for aren't as easy to write as it seems, especially if you want to be "anatomically correct". The first rule ever would be knowing what you're writing about! So, if you happen not to be a male, you'll need to be careful on how you end up writing the sex scene and how accurate to real life it is. Unless you're writing something belonging to the Omegaverse, odds are that you'll need to make your research.

So, I know it might be scary but it would be a good idea to ask to your friends. Fortunately for me I do have gay friends who are super happy to guide me into the dos and don'ts. The last thing in the Universe for me it's to represent something in a bad light and make things worse! (We're not in the 70s or 90s anymore!)

Another idea is to read a bunch of good literature! Not only yaoi manga but also LGBTQ+ young adult and adult novels out there. The more you read, the better. And please: don't stop reading because it will keep you inspired.

It's also a good idea to get feedback and be open to the feedback. You can share your work in the Yaoi forums here on dePepi. You can also ask feedback to your friends, or share under a nickname so that you can become comfy with it.

That being said: if you're not sure about what you're writing about, better to "insinuate" that things are happening without the need of describing the deed. Sometimes that will work better than just trying to be super artistic! It all comes down to knowing anatomy, knowing what's possible and what's not, and being nice while writing the scenes. And if you're not sure about it: avoid! Because the worse thing ever is a badly written sex scene. (We can actually forgive anything else but this).

OKAY, FANTASTIC, BUT HOW CAN I STEAM THINGS UP WITHOUT DESCRIBING ANYTHING THEN?

You can create the tension and use language and images to imply that they had sex. Let's see some examples from the film industry:

North by Northwest (1959)

In Alfred Hitchcock's North by Northwest we have a couple, a train and a tunnel. The couple of protagonists kiss while traveling in a train which enters a tunnel. I think this one is pretty easy to grasp of what is point out at what's happening with that couple.

Blow-up (1966)

In Blow Up we have a photographer taking pictures and getting more and more sweaty. So much so that he seems almost out of breath. The model is also more alluring and making more sexy poses. But when the photographer finishes the roll, he collapses exhausted on a coach, almost as if he had been running a marathon!

By showing the photographer going all sweaty and being all focussed on each of the poses of the model, we get a great sexy representation to spark the imagination of the viewer without needing to describe in depth as it would happen with erotica.

Un Chant d'Amour (1950)

In Jean Genet's Un Chant d'Amour we find two prisoners, one in each cell, sharing a wall and tons of sexual tension between them. There's a ward, and he seems jealous and tries to stop them. However, the two men, still in their cells, keep at it. So, what do they do? A hole between their cells where they blow some smoke from a cigarette and they suck it from the other end!

There's still a wall between them, they still cannot touch, but the image is so compelling that your imagination ends up steaming up greatly.

So, you see, you can get creative implying that something is happening. In fact, doing so you might even enhance your readers imagination and make their minds blow away! It's also a cool way of "torturing" a bit your readers while also sparking their imagination and saving the steam for one big scene within the book. You can also hint at something happening but not the whole thing and you can effectively have people swooning and shipping the couple for not only a book but many! (Please read the Court of Thorns and Roses series of Sarah J. Maas to get a great example of this).

EROTICA

If you're going to write erotica, whatever the combination and the detail you want to show in scenes, please be mindful and make it real. This means that if you haven't had the pleasure yet to sweat alongside your sweetheart, please do research human anatomy. Unfortunately, magic won't make the trick, especially if what you write is unbelievable.

Readers want to dream, but they also want to find parts of themselves in the characters they love. Having something utterly impossible might have exactly the opposite effect of what you intend. There's nothing worse than bad erotica!

Also, using as research porn as an only source is a big mistake. While porn can help you, it won't show you the warmth that many readers might want to read. True, if you want to focus only on the steam you might get away with it, but you'd be writing a one shot. If you aim for a series, readers will be hooked on feelings and the drama around the characters and enjoy steam, but steam alone won't make it for them to keep reading.

Aim for a series, leave the writing practice for fan fiction forums. Practice online and get the skills you need to create stories that your readers won't be able to put down.

TWENTY-ONE
ELEMENTS OF STYLE

Style is not the fashion you wear, but the way you present yourself to the world. In literary terms, it's how the words you use will create the character of the whole book. Is it witty? Funny? Steamy? Suspenseful? What will make your story unique will be the style you give to it; in other words, your style.

TONE

If your story is light, then you want to write "marshmallows". If your story is steamy, then you want to write "spicy food". These are just easy examples on how the tone can be; you make the rules as long as you follow them. It means that you have to be consistent throughout the book to make it work.

Also, description as super as long as they're not boring. "Show, don't tell" is the way to make things pop up and spark the imagination of your readers. Funny scenes are also cool, but don't overpopulate the book with scenes that don't advance the story because the story might feel stagnant. Scenes should always advance the plot.

Whatever the tone you choose to use, please make yourself a favor: be consistent. It'll make your readers be taken by the story and recognize your writings as well.

POV

POV stands for "point of view". You can explain your stories from many perspectives, and that will also change the character and tone of the book. You can write in the first person (I wrote a book) or the third person (she read a book).

Many romance novels are written in the first person. It's more intimate and it feels like you're friends with the main character. In a sense, you're "channeling the character" and it can be a little bit challenging because, as actors and actresses do, to be consistent, you need to remain in character. It can be super tricky on how you present the information as well (in dialogues and descriptions).

The first person is intimate, has a confessional tone, and readers are more likely to empathize with the main character. However, it's also very limiting and it's easy to become messy.

You can also use the "multiple first person". This happens when, for example, in one chapter you have one character as the main, and then the next, you have another character. If the tone isn't done correctly, readers could be confused on who is talking each time. Also, you might have less time to empathize with each of the characters.

Then you have the third person who knowns everything, aka "God". This is a versatile way of writing since you can move from one character to another character easily maintaining the tone (with exception of the dialogues when each of the characters show up as themselves). Also, you get to know more about the world and the characters. On the downfall, readers will not have the same level of intimacy with the characters as if you used the first person.

TENSE

You can write your book in the present tense, or in the passed tense. The present is fresh and full of energy. Things happen immediately one after the other. On the other hand, the past is static, a memory, a reflection.

You can always combine the two, but don't do it too often because it can be confusing for the reader.

The most important part is to be consistent. Whatever your choices are, from names to tenses, you need to always be consistent.

PART THREE
SELF-PUBLISHING

TWENTY-TWO
WHERE TO PLACE YOUR BL NOVEL IN THE KINDLE STORE

Amazon places ebooks in virtual shelves. Amazon's Kindle Store is a massive search engine, not really a book store. For every purchase made on Kindle Books, Amazon makes cash. It means that if you place your book in the correct shelf, you'll be most likely to be successful.

Romance is an umbrella for many different romance sub-genres. This is good news, because each sub-genre sits into subcategories. Each of these help you to get on the top of the niche.

In the UK Kindle Store, you get have a main umbrella, Romance, with over 50 subcategories. The good news is that new subcategories are appearing all the time. And the bad news is that some do disappear. The trick is to place your book in the right one to get into the top of the list for the Amazon's algorithm to recommend it to new readers and to appear on the top searches.

There're 28 main categories on Amazon, where romance themes can be found all over.

1. Arts & Photography
2. Biography & True Accounts
3. Business & Investing
4. Children's eBooks

5. Comics, Manga & Graphic Novels
6. Computing
7. Crime, Thriller & Mystery
8. Education & Reference
9. Food & Drink
10. Health & Fitness
11. History
12. Home & Garden
13. Humour
14. LGBTQ+
15. Literature & Fiction
16. Nonfiction
17. Parenting & Families
18. Politics & Social Sciences
19. Professional & Technical
20. Religion & Spirituality
21. Romance
22. Science & Maths
23. Science Fiction & Fantasy
24. Self-Help & Counselling
25. Sport
26. Teen & Young Adult
27. Travel & Tourism
28. eBooks in Foreign Languages

Within the Romance Kindle category we get 17 main subcategories:

Books> Romance>

1. Collections & Anthologies
2. Contemporary
3. Fantasy
4. Gay Romance
5. Gothic
6. Historical Romance

7. Lesbian Romance
8. Military
9. New Adult
10. Paranormal
11. Religious
12. Romance
13. Romantic Comedy
14. Romantic Suspense
15. Science Fiction
16. Time Travel
17. Westerns

If we click on "Books> Romance> Romance>" we'll find other shelves where we can put our book. For example, following that path we'll land within the umbrella of "literature & fiction" and there we'll find 11 other sub-sub-sub-categories where we can place our book.

‹ Literature & Fiction

1. Action & Adventure
2. Adventure
3. Crime, Thrillers & Mystery
4. Fantasy
5. LGBTQ+
6. Men's Adventure
7. Romance
8. Short Stories
9. Travel
10. War & Military
11. Women's Adventure

The list does not stop here since you can find almost 50 sub-categories within fantasy and science fiction, at least eight sub-categories within teen and young adult, and more!

As you can see, there're many different categories, sub-categories, and sub-sub-categories where you can effectively place your book.

WHAT DOES THIS MEAN?

It means that if you research categories carefully, you'll find a niche (a small one) where you can place your book on the top sellers.

Amazon assigns an "Amazon best seller rank", aka ABSR, number to each book based on the number of sales per day on the Amazon market. For example, if you have a 100 ABSR, it means that there're other 99 books that are performing better than yours. The lowest the ABSR number, the better your book is performing. Hence, choosing the right categories for your book is paramount to achieve the top in the list.

By choosing some categories where your book would fit and researching the numbers on the Kindlepreneur Kindle Sales Rank Calculator (https://kindlepreneur.com/amazon-kdp-sales-rank-calculator/) you can figure out where your book might perform better and how many books per day you need to sell to achieve that.

Best Sellers Rank: 2,527 in Kindle Store (See Top 100 in Kindle Store)
1 in LGBTQ+ Adventure Fiction
47 in Action & Adventure Romance Fiction
88 in Holiday Fiction (Kindle Store)

For example, if you choose a category where the number 1 book on the list has an ABSR of 2,527; it means that you need to sell over 79 books per day to reach that.

```
Best Sellers Rank: 222 in Kindle Store (See Top 100 in Kindle Store)
    1 in Lesbian Fiction
    2 in LGBTQ+ Literature & Fiction (Books)
    4 in War Story Fiction
```

However, if you choose a category where the number 1 book on the list has an ABSR of 222; it means that you need to sell over 462 books per day to reach the target.

```
Best Sellers Rank: 7,666 in Kindle Store (See Top 100 in Kindle Store)
    1 in LGBTQ+ Nonfiction
    2 in Australian & Oceanian History
    3 in Countries & Regions of Australasia & Pacific
```

So, if you choose a category where the number 1 book on the list has an ABSR of 7,999; it means that you have to sell over 20 books a day to meet the target.

Hence, the category you choose has a direct effect on whether you'll become an Amazon Best Seller and if you'll be able to market yourself as such.

NOW THE BIG QUESTION IS: WHAT IS YOUR NICHE? Because you'll be self-publishing, you have to be clear about the category and sub-category where you want to place your book. Wherever you place it, you'll be competing with similar books. Try to avoid general placements, and instead place your book in niches that are more or less hot. For example, if you have written a romance where one of the characters is a werewolf, then you need to choose the right subcategory for it: romance > paranormal > werewolves.

One o the reasons to place your book in small niches is "discoverability". It's going to be easier to be found in a niche than in a broader category! I would not recommend to write for the market, but once you've written a story that you love, then you can see where you can effectively place it.

So, if you want to help your reader to find your book, then you need to understand clearly where it would need to be placed first. So, your target is to be strategic and place your book in a niche where it can thrive. It means that the subcategory cannot be too broad nor too small where you cannot achieve anything. You want to book to rank within a subcategory so that you can then market it as a top-seller.

Ranking on the top in the Kindle Store will allow your book to be discovered in an organic way. Why do you want that? Because once you've made the initial effort to market your book, it'll roll almost alone! If marketing roles alone and in an organic way, it means that you won't need to focus on that book and will be able to focus on a new one.

WRITING TO MARKET

This brings the issue of wanting to write to market. It's a very yummy cookie, however it will only work if the niche you are good at it's the same that's hot beans now. Although some niches are on the rise, like werewolves, others that might seem interesting to target at the moment might disappear at any time.

That the niche might disappear next year is not the main issue here, but the vibe in your writing. If you like what you write it will show. However, if you write just because you want to get the cash, then it will certainly not work. If you enjoy what you write, it will show. Believe me.

A testament to writing something just for fun is my first ever self-published book Geek Anthropology of Loki's Army.

I spent over a year just researching Marvel's fandom for sheer fun. One of the main reasons for that is being a fan myself. Then, I decided to write a book analyzing the fandom of Loki, because why not! The result is a long book of "fan-girling" from the perspective of anthropology. I can assure you that the number of searches on the matter is low, and yet I had loads of fun by writing it and also learnt a lot by self-publishing it.

My memories of researching, writing and then self-publishing the book are very dear to me. In fact, I made lots of friends because of it! If I had decided to writing to market I would have never written this book!

I'm not saying not to do it, but only to refrain if the niche to choose is something you don't like at all. The funny thing is that despite the book being weird to the core, it does bring monthly residuals.

HOW COMPETITIVE IS YOUR NICHE?

Now, if you enjoy what you write, the next question is: how competitive is your niche? You'll need to take a look at what you love to read and write, and where it's placed in the Kindle Store. So, what you need to do is to see how many books have been published in that particular category, which will hint to the demand of similar types of books.

To understand how your book will compete with the rest, you need to take a look at the ranking of the books in that category. In Amazon, go to the drop-down menu for the Kindle Store, then Kindle eBooks tab, and then choose bestsellers.

Click on the main category where your book wold be located and take a look at what type of books appear in it. Then, do the same with subcategories. Then, notice the book at the top, the book on the 100th position. Use the Kindlepreneur Kindle Sales Rank Calculator (https://kindlepreneur.com/amazon-kdp-sales-rank-calculator/) and start making out the categories that will best fit your book while at the same time will bring more possibilities for you to hit the top on the list.

Please notice that rankings are continuously being updated. Hence, it's paramount that you check the data during a few days to build an idea on the possibilities of your book.

We'll also need an estimate of the number of books in a certain niche. The number should appear on the top o the page. Once you get the idea, then you can see where to better place your book. The trick will be to use keywords related to that category! (That's why it's a super cool idea to write the description of the book and the blurb after doing a bit of a research).

BE SMART: DON'T CHOOSE TOO CROWDED

To make it to the number one in the list for that category, you should choose a niche which isn't as crowded. And since you can list your book in two different categories, you can use one to rank on the top your book, and the other one to slowly go up in the rank. The second option should be where your book fits the best. However, the smaller niche cannot be random. Remember that readers will be happier and leave better reviews if everything matches.

So, you should have two categories where one will give you the ranking, and the second where your book will be a perfect match and can slowly become a hit.

Go to the Kindlepreneur Kindle Sales Rank Calculator (https://kindlepreneur.com/amazon-kdp-sales-rank-calculator/) and make some research. For example, a book ranking 200 is selling around 500 books per day, and a book ranking 6,000 is selling 24 books per day.

Small niches can bring you modest earnings but also a chance to grow your readership. The more books you self-publish, the more you'll sell. But if you place them in the wrong shelve, odds are that your books will never be discovered. Hence, it's paramount to spend some time in the Kindle Store looking at categories and building a strategy.

HOW TO FIND THE PERFECT AMAZON CATEGORY FOR YOUR BOOK

Go to the search feature on Amazon and start typing the combinations of words that you think would fit your book. You'll find similar books to you and you'll find out their categories and ranking number.

Go to the books from the top to the bottom of the list taking notes of their category strings. In that way you'll see which categories fit best, where you can become a best seller and what other hidden sub-categories Amazon has placed those books. (Astonishing but true, Amazon doesn't list all the categories in a visible way).

> **Best Sellers Rank:** 30 in Kindle Store (See Top 100 in Kindle Store)
> 3 in Romantic Suspense (Books)
> 4 in Romantic Suspense (Kindle Store)
> 5 in Contemporary Romance (Kindle Store)

Once you've found the categories that best tune with your book, check the number 1 best seller in those categories. Copy their ABSR ranking number and then use the calculator to know how many books per day they're selling.

Once you've got a list of categories, narrow it down to the ones that most represent your book. Then use the Kindlepreneur calculator to see which one is the best for you to target as a main category (https://kindlepreneur.com/amazon-kdp-sales-rank-calculator/).

If you also want to publish a paperback, to the same thing but with paperback versions. Ebooks and paperbacks, even if these are two different versions of the same book, might be indeed performing in a different way in Amazon.

SO, HOW MANY CATEGORIES ARE IN AMAZON?

Amazon has more than 15,000 different categories. Unfortunately, Amazon doesn't show all the categories. So, the research might take you some hours to do it effectively. However, if you've spent some months writing a very nice book, it's worth researching where to place your book in the Kindle Store to be successful.

If you have some more budget, you can choose "Publisher Rocket" to find the keywords for you (https://depepi--rocket.thrivecart.com/publisher-rocket/ - affiliate link, don't worry, you don't pay any extras). It will see you time and you will be able to check more categories and keywords in a shorter period of time.

Publisher Rocket has a very easy interface and it. You just need to check out the combination of words that you want to explore. Publisher Rocket will give you a list of items, where the green colored ones are the good options. For example, for "yaoi manga English paperback" you get a niche were you can thrive.

Also, you can take a look at the competitors closer with just some clicks and see how they're performing.

TWENTY-THREE
SHORT FICTION IN THE KINDLE STORE

Not all of us are prepare to read a 500-page novel. Many of us just read a bit every day and prefer books that won't take us ages. Instead of planning a long book, why not think of it as a series?

Short stories go from a minimum of 3,000 words up to 8,000. Novellas range from 20,000 up to 40,000; and a short romance novel goes from 40,000 words. This is good news since most non-self-published novels start at 60,000 words. The advantages of writing shorter books is that you can create badass series and release more books that can be read in some days while going and coming from work in a bus or a train. Not everyone out there can spend hours on reading!

On top of that, many people are book hoarders and Kindle devices are making that even easier. Hence, consuming shorter ebooks are making it easy to satisfy romance readers' thirst for more stories. Thus, short fiction is perfect to enjoy reading for those who have just a bit of free time. Short stories are also a great way to make yourself known and for readers to get hooked on your stories.

Your book will be classified according to the number of words of your story. The "word-count" will determine what your story will be: a novella? A short novel? In the Kindle Store you can find Short

Reads. Many readers go to fish their kick there are are eager to pay cheaply to consume many stories and series. The Kindle Store also gives an average of minutes for short stories. For example, a novella usually reads in two or three hours, which makes it perfect for commuting to work and enjoy during the week. See where I'm going?

A novella rounds around 100 pages. If that's too short for your story, 200 pages will work well too. Remember to go to the Kindle Store and use some time to research the books in your category: how long are these? How do the books at the top look like? How do the covers look like? How are authors promoting these books?

Amazon will assign your book automatically to a virtual shelf depending on the number of pages. Hence, if you want to make sure Amazon will place your book where you want, take care of its length. For example, if your book is 400 pages, why not making a series?

What's more, if you use any romance trope, you can also use it to place your book in the right virtual shelf. For example, if your book has a millionaire protagonist you might want to place your book into the wealthy heroes area. The combination of main categories and short reads will give you a bigger chance to get discovered by your readers.

THE PERKS OF WRITING 30K-WORD BOOKS

Writing novellas or "short books" is a blessing and your readers will love you for giving them a good bust of feelings.

- Your readers will finish the whole story and feel happy with it. As we stablished, not everybody has a lot of time to dedicate their time to 500 pages. However, short stories in a series will give your readers the bust they crave when finishing a story. Please think about those

times when you finish a book and you feel fulfilled. You get the picture.
- You're also giving your readers the chance to reach for the new read in the series. Yup: I just said the next read in the series! I you have the material to write a book of 600 pages, why not writing a duopoly instead? Or better still, three books in a series?
- This is also a great way to try new genres for you! You can write sci-fi romance or fantasy romance or even mystery romance! Test your limits while writing short novels!
- Short stories also give you a great way to get to know your readers better too. They will like to know what's next for you as well. Hint: you should start thinking about a newsletter.

TWENTY-FOUR
KEYWORDS, CATEGORIES, THE FEARED BOOK DESCRIPTION & BLURB

To start publishing on Kindle books, you need to create an account on Amazon KDP. First, create your account and then follow the instructions and create and upload your fantastic romance BL novel to Kindle books.

You need to complete all steps. Remember to click input all the information on the series section if you plan to create a series. You can always return to this page and update the book (or the series), so don't worry if you don't have things super clear the first time.

However, there's something you need to explore while you're writing your book and that will help your book being a great hit: keywords, categories and the book description.

You'll need to optimize the book details for self-publishing in the Kindle bookstore. The important thing to remember is that Amazon is a massive search engine. As such, you need to hit on the right keywords and categories where to place your book so readers can find it easily.

You need to help Amazon recognize that your book is selling very well, so the engine will also help you sell more books. Amazon uses "hot releases" lists where they promote those hot books that the Amazon algorithm catches as attractive due to being on the top in their niches. It does that by using keywords in your book title and description. Hence, you need to embed those keywords exactly there!

This is good news and also bad news because on the one hand Amazon helps you doing the marketing, but also it means that you have limited control over it. The Kindle Store will put your book into a virtual shelf, and you need to be super clear on which one you'd like to be into for magic to happen.

Since Amazon will only make money if you sell books, the engine will promote more the books that are bringing in the cash. So, it's in your best interest to find the best keywords to help your readers find your book and Amazon promote it.

Keywords are words that readers use to find your book. (It works very much like when you look for stuff in Google). So, it's super important that you allow yourself some time to research the keywords that you think are the ones and then explore Amazon and see what's happening to similar books to yours.

Something similar happens with the book description, the subtitles and the blurb that you place on the back cover of your magnificent creation. I need to create expectation so that the reader will click and buy the book. The game of keywords embedded while creating emotional want are the key for us buying the book. While the book cover will be the first appeal into reading the blurb, the description you place there will be what will make your readers ending up purchasing your book or not.

Imaging the blurb and the description as a short sales pitch. You need to show that the book is worth the time of the reader, that they'll have a great time and loads of entertainment reading your book. And remember to embed in the description the keywords that the Amazon algorithm will use to place your book in the correct shelf too.

While your book might have been a work of months, and while you might be super exited and eager to self-publish right away, you need to spend some time researching keywords, categories and finding out if similar books are having a blast in that specific shelf. Then, you need to also spend some time to create a killer blurb.

The most important question here for you will be: how can I help my readers find my book?

Once you have the answer to that question, then ask yourself: would I buy my own book if I read this blurb I've written? (If the answer is no, then take some more time writing the description and the blurb!)

Amazon only will allow you to type seven keywords or combinations of keywords. As we've mentioned, the key is to use those keywords in your subtitle (or title if you wish) and your book description. Always remember to make it natural.

Think about yourself: how do you search for new books on Amazon? Do you usually use one keyword or do you use a combination of them? It's most likely to use strings of keywords. Hence, try to research the best ones for you. There's only a catch: some categories do have requirements within the Kindle Store. You will also find tips and best practices. I do recommend taking a look at: https://kdp.amazon.com/en_US/help/topic/G201298500

Keywords will help you with the organic search. If you place keywords in your title or the subtitle and the book description, you're good to go!

Remember: you can choose two categories for each book. Hence, if you choose a main category and then a niche category, you have more chances to make your book easily found and easier to reach the top list in the niche you've chosen.

You can skip all the manual labor with Publisher Rocket https://depepi--rocket.thrivecart.com/publisher-rocket/

(affiliate link; don't worry, there're no extras for you). You can certainly find the keywords you need manually, but it might take as many hours as the ones you need to write your book. Or you can such get your Publisher Rocket license and be quicker. It's up to you (and your pocket).

TWENTY-FIVE
GIVE YOUR BOOK A PRICE!

Pricing is not my forte. Fortunately, if you're like me, Amazon will help you greatly. You can keep a 70% of books priced between $2.99 and $9.99 and a 35% for those prized less. Also, if you take a look at the price of those books in the niche where you want to place yours, you'll get a good idea. (To me it's a blessing that you can figure out how to price your book like this, otherwise I'd have a long headache and even nightmares with it!)

Once you know who your audience is and what they're used to pay to read books (hint: research the other books in your niche), and how much authors price similar books to yours, you will find out the price range in your category. Once you get that, you can choose to price yours too.

Usually, a short story or a novella go from $0.99 to $2.99. However, this might change depending on the niche. That's why it's very important to check. You can also choose to enroll your book in Kindle Select. There's only a problem: Amazon demands exclusivity for 90 days. So, if you're thinking about self-publishing in other platforms like Kobo or Apple books, then you should not choose Kindle Select.

I have one book in Kindle Select which belongs to a super niche category. I wrote it just for the fun of it and decided to enroll it in Kindle Select to see what happens. What I discovered is that, even with books that are so arcane, you can have benefits. However, this might not be a good idea for all of your books. Again, this is mostly a question of researching and even testing.

If you use Publisher Rocket (https://depepi--rocket.thrivecart.com/publisher-rocket/ - affiliate link), you can also research the price of the books in your same niche. If you price your book too cheaply, you're damaging your niche! If you price your book too much, then you're damaging yourself.

Average Price

$ 13

$ 8

$ 12

Publisher Rocket will give you a price for every combination of words you're researching. You should go along with the average price (or a little bit lower, but not much - please, don't smash the market!)

Readers will be used to that price-range, and this makes things easier for you if you have no idea how to price your book!

TWENTY-SIX
E-BOOKS AND PAPERBACKS

You can also print your book through KDP Print Paperbacks. I didn't choose this option with my first book because I wanted to explore other options. What can I say? I'm a curious creature and I like to tinker and test stuff.

Once you've published your ebook, you can also start thinking about self-publishing a paperback through Amazon. It's cool because Amazon can give you an ISBN and they can print it for you once people request a copy (print-on-demand!)

Some readers love paperbacks more than ebooks. Others just buy paperbacks of their favorite books. So, having a paperback version of your book is a great idea as well. Unlike the ebook, changes are not automatic and you might need purchasing a new copy of the book to see if you got it right.

Having a printed version of your ebook will also allow you to take pictures of it and use it for marketing purposes. You will also be able to offer the same book in different formats and priced in different ways. Many people might find your book as a paperback but feel more compelled to buy the ebook once they see there's a more expensive version of it!

The only downfall is that you'll need to re-design the cover and then ask some copies to see that the quality is good. So, my advice to you is to first publish the ebook, and then the paperback so you will also have an excuse to market you book again. If you do mind who the publisher is, don't use Amazon's free ISBN. Instead, you'll need to purchase your own. Don't worry, Amazon doesn't ask exclusivity for printed books, you can create another edition elsewhere too.

Find more information on KDP here: https://kdp.amazon.com/en_US/help/topic/GHKDSCW2KQ3K4UU4

TWENTY-SEVEN
CREATE YOUR AMAZING COVER

The cover can certainly be an issue. All can be for nothing if the cover of your book isn't flashy enough. One way to go is to purchase an already made cover. You can find those by looking on Google.

However, if you're in a tight budget or you're not eager to pay much, you can create one for free using Canva, just like I did. You can find many nice examples of Canva and you can also get inspired by taking a look at all the books in the Kindle Store that are already in the category where you'll place your book.

It took me weeks to find a version of a version of the cover I loved. In my personal case, I didn't ask anything to anyone else. I was just picky and until I created something cute that catches my eyes, I didn't stop.

After creating my favorite cover and also some other versions of it, I asked my friends which one they preferred. You already know which one they loved!

The most expensive version is to hire a professional to create the cover of your book. If you do have a friend who draws well, you can come up with an arrangement or perhaps better price options. This is what happened with my first self-published book on the Kindle Store.

CREATE YOUR AMAZING COVER   113

GEEK ANTHROPOLOGY
OF LOKI'S ARMY
BY PEPI VALDERRAMA

If you do, please remember to mention the author of the illustration! Don't just add it there and forget about how it happened. It's not only good manners, it's also the good way to go. (And if you are wondering, at the time I was super on all things Loki and my hair was very orange).

TWENTY-EIGHT
MARKETING ROMANCE

You should be announcing the lunch of your book within two or three weeks before it gets live on the Kindle Store. To do that, you'll need to set up a date and keep the plan going.

It's a hard thing to do, believe, but you'll also need to plan to what to share and when on your social media. I would also recommend to start building a Newsletter if you're planning to write and launch more books.

Most people make a calculation of how long it takes for them to write a book and work with the pressure. I'm more the type of having the draft prepared and the cover, and have the book waiting to publish on the Kindle Store. Choose what works best for you, just remember not to end up procrastinating or not meeting your own deadlines if you promised them on your social media or to all your Newsletter list!

I use Buffer to plan what I share in social media. I usually share on Instagram and sometimes on Facebook. It allows me to plan some weeks in advance.

I also use some Apps that help me create nice pictures to share information in a nice manner. CC Express and Prequel can help you create amazing graphics and share your book's information.

Sending out a Newsletter from time to time is also a good idea while you're building a nice readership for your books.

I also use MailChimp for my shy Newsletter. I'm not a fan of receiving too many Newsletters myself. Hence I'm super careful on what I do send out. Also, I don't want people to forget me. For me, once a month works at the moment. And if I have something extra to share, then it's once every two weeks. However, "spamming" folk with too many newsletters is not a good idea. Refrain sharing too much and being too pushy. The last thing you want to do is to spam people.

The challenge here is to prepare a launch marketing plan for three weeks and once the book has launched, allow two weeks to see how it's going. Then assess what's working and what's not working. You might need changing the description of the book, or how you approach future books of the series (if the first one belongs to the series).

Take the first and the second book you self-publish as testing grounds and then tinker until you find your perfect niche.

How to market romance for two weeks then? Well, you should start sharing on social media before those three weeks in a sheepish way. Once you enter into the three weeks arena, I would recommend to start sharing about your book once every day (or two days). For that you'll need to prepare all the graphics and writing!

I know, this is quite a lot of work considering you'll be on your own. However, it's highly rewarding. You don't need to share a bible with each picture on Instagram. You only need to make things hot for you. And if that doesn't have too much feedback, don't despair because Amazon will help you too.

Unfortunately, there's no magic way of making things work but to research and then tinker what best works for you.

———

EXAMPLE OF BOOK LAUNCH MARKETING GOODNESS

You don't need to follow the following steps if you don't want to, but here you have an example of what you can use as a marketing strategy when launching your wonderful BL book.

- WHILE YOU'RE STILL WRITING: try to build an ARC (advanced readers' copy) group. If you already have a newsletter is easy. However, if you don't you can always try to find ARC readers on social media. If you aren't lucky, then you can always ask your family.
- ASK YOUR ARC READERS TO LEAVE A REVIEW: because you'll give them a free copy of your book, you can certainly ask for some reviews as an exchange. Be aware that not all reviews will be positive ones.
- MAKE A COVER REVEAL: once you have designed your cover, use it as a marketing device and share it with the world in social media. If you're like me, you can ask for ARC readers at the same time as you show off your fantastic new book cover.
- SET UP A PRICE: this can be after a month or as little as a week after knowing the launching date. Let your ARC readers know all about the price and the laughing date so they'll be able to leave some reviews for you.
- THANK YOUR ARC READERS: always thank people that help you! Even if it's just a simple email, do it. (It's better if you add some little digital perks to it).
- CREATE HYPE WITH PAID ADS: if you do have the budget, consider to create an ad through Amazon Ads or BookBub Ads.
- MEET YOUR AUDIENCE ON INSTAGRAM: if you're chatty, why not meeting your audience on Instagram (or any other platform that allows you to meet your readers online) and stream Live a Q&A event? You can share

more about the story with your readers and they'll feel closer to you as well.
- PRICE TACTICS: price your book cheaper for some weeks so you will get more sales. Also make sure that Amazon placed you in the right categories for your book.
- USE YOUR BOOK TO PROMOTE YOUR BOOK! This might sound obvious, but many people always forget to use their own book to create amazing social media banners and posts. Show off!

PART FOUR
EXTRAS

TWENTY-NINE
MAIN BL/YAOI/801 WORDS

So, yaoi or BL are umbrella terms for the genre. If you want to be picky, you can use yaoi only for sex-centered stories, and BL for story-centered manga. And if you're going to be even pickier, go to the depths of the words.

Yaoi: acronym that comes from 「ヤマなし、オチなし、イミなし」 (**ya**ma nashi, **o**chi nashi, **i**mi nashi), or "no climax, no punch line, no sense." It kind of refers to stories that without sex wouldn't have any meaning. Some fans, however, have re-interpreted the acronym. Instead, they argue it comes from 「やめて、お尻が痛い！」 (**ya**mete, **o**shiri ga **i**tai!), or "stop, my butt hurts!" This ironic statement might be connected to one of the most prevalent tropes in the genre: romantiziced non-consesual sex. You'll find out that many stories depict non-consensual sex as precursor of a loving relationship.

801: is *yaoi* written with numbers. In Japanese, you can write words with numbers by taking into consideration the pronunciation of the numbers. Eight is "ya" or "hachi," zero can be also an "o" and read as an "o," and one can be "i" or "ichi." It feels like a code, but since you can find this type of word-number play virtually everywhere, anyone can read it.

Bara: 「バラ」, or rose, refers to hyper-sexualized and very graphic yaoi stories. These usually aren't directed to a female audience but to a gay male one. Beware, because "bara" is also used by the gay subculture. Thus, "bara" might only mean "gay culture" as a whole.

Shonen-Ai: 「少年愛」 is basically BL. However, stories are more focussed on romance and not sex. Hence, there's a great focus on the feelings and the story. And even if sex is happening in closed doors, the manga will show little of it.

Now that we're savvy about the most essential words regarding the genre. Let's take a look at the readers. Fans use different words to point at themselves. Usually, these type of words are sweet and cute. However, in BL fans decided to take irony (and maybe also shame) into account when choosing what to use as a word for themselves.

Fujoshi/ Fudanshi: it's the general word for the girls/boys that love BL. Fujoshi or 「腐女子」 is used for girls, while fudanshi 「腐男子」 is used for boys. It literally means rotten girl/boy. The terms were born as a form of self-deprecation. Admiring or liking BL is a type of rotting thing, hence the use of 「腐す」 "kusasu," to rot, to speak ill of something. That kanji is also the one for Tofu, that yummy Japanese delicatessen that vegetarians and vegans love. So, it isn't that bad after all.

Because of the rotting composition of the word, some fans like to call themselves "Fenix." Others prefer 「貴腐人」 "gifujin," because it's more agendered, but that one isn't less deprecating. And some male fans also use 「腐兄」 "fukei," which is also quite ironic. As long as you have the rotting kanji somewhere, the irony and self-deprecation are present.

So, now that we know the essential words for the genre and the fans what about the characters? Broadly speaking there are three: the dominant, the submissive, and the switch. And yes, it does sound a lot like entering the arena of BDSM.

Seme: 「攻め」 is the dominant one in a BL couple. It's a quite graphic way to point at the dominant homosexual partner since the verb "semeru" means to attack. However, this is one of the many words that we can use for the dominant guy. Others include "Tachi" 「タチ」 and "hidarigawa" 「左側」 (literally, "left side.")

To call someone seme is just using a general term. Some characters have others quirks. In that case, we can find words like "souseme" 「総攻め」 perfect dominant, "tachisen" 「タチ専」 or complete dominant (as a fetish, basically), and "dakisen" 「抱き専」 or clingy seme (he likes to embrace a lot.) But wait, there're more sub-types of seme!

SUPER SEME-SAMA: 「スーパー攻め様」 is the quintessential type of seme. He's stylish, good-looking, confident, and super manly. But it's also serious and wants to do his way all the time, even if it means doing it by force.

(Super Seme-Sama example: Asami from the Finder series by Ayane Yamano).

KOTOBA SEME: 「言葉攻め」 is a dominant guy that likes to play with words while doing it with his partner. He usually whispers all types of obscene words and insults to make him hotter than he is at the moment.

KEIGO SEME: 「敬語攻め」 is a dominant guy that likes to be super polite while doing it and uses honorific words while they're making love.

AYAMARI SEME: 「謝り攻め」 is a seme that uses excuses and apologies while they're at it. It can be that the seme knows that he's doing the wrong thing and he's apologizing while he's forcing his partner.

Uke: 「受け」 is the submissive partner in a homosexual relationship. The word is also pretty descriptive since it comes from the verb "ukeru" or to receive. There are other words to call the uke, for example, "Neko" 「ネコ」 cat, and "migigawa" 「右側」 which literally means "right side."

When the guy is always an uke regardless of the partner, we're talking about a perfect uke, or "sou uke" 「総受け」. But, as happens with the seme, there're many other sub-types of ukes.

INRAN UKE: 「淫乱受け」 is an uke who is eager to do it at any time. He's lascivious, wild, and lewd. It can also be that the uke is profoundly affected by the sexual relationship with his current partner.

Joou-sama Uke: 「女王様受け」 means "princess uke." This type of uke is mean. They're beautiful, but they show off in a pompous manner because they know they're like queens for the seme. They have power or authority over the seme. And they can be oppressive and extremely mean. But, the seme are so in love that they let them do whatever they want.

Bitch: 「ビッチ」 is an uke that has a very disordered sex life or one that has many partners. Or it could be a very sad uke that ends up having lots of sex just because he feels very lonely. Please note the word is only used with ukes. And yes, it can come as very deprecating since there's an equivalent with women. Welcome to the trope world of BL manga.

Seke: 「セケ」 or switch. A "seke" is someone who will be a seme or an uke depending on the partner, or even with the current partner. They like to do everything.

Now that we have the type of characters, we need to take a look at the words referring to the couples. In yaoi, there're different types of couples. However, the main word to say couple in Japanese is just "coupling."

Coupling: 「カップリング」 aka shipping or pairing. This word can be shortened as only CP, or "kapu." However, couples or ships are best known for saying the names of the characters using an x in the middle. For example, Thor x Loki. But, you can shorten that by using a combination of the names. In this case, we'd call this ship Thorki. It's pretty straightforward, isn't it?

Sub-Cup: 「サブカプ」 aka sub-couple is short for a secondary ship that might appear in the BL manga. While some fans can go crazy with the first couple, others might swoon for the sub-couple.

Riba: 「リバ」 is the short version of "reversible couple." It's a ship where both uke and seme exchange roles in their relationship. This is quite an egalitarian coupling.

Yuripple: 「百合ッブル」 is a ship where there are two ukes.

Both love one another, and both are ukes. "Yuri" comes from the Girls Love arena, where "yuri" means "lily."

Seme-seme/ kou-kou: 「攻x攻」 is a ship where two semes love each other. They might even take turns to be the uke, but they are in endless competition. Because they're rivals and they love each other, the problems in the coupling are secured. Hence, the appeal for this type of coupling.

Words to Call Each Other

We're going to also take a look at what the lovebirds might call each other. Although each manga will show different ways, there is a general convention on how semes and ukes might call each other.

Muko: 「婿」 means husband or groom. So, if an uke calls "my husband" to his partner, he's affectionate. It can also be that fans use the word "muko" to point out who the dominant partner might be in the ship without using the words seme or tachi.

Yome: 「嫁」 means wife or bride. If a seme calls "my wife" to his uke, then he's affectionate (or ironic, depending on the manga). It can also be that the fans are using "yome" to point out who the passive partner might be in a coupling without using the words uke or neko.

Honorable Mentions

And, finally, here we have some honorable mentions:

Age gap coupling: when the age gap between the seme and uke is substantial.

Bishonen: aka "bishies," are very good-looking men.

Crack Ship/Pairing: is a type of extreme shipping. It happens when fans ship impossible couples, that most probably kill each other than make sex together. It can also be that the ship is so far away from the official canon that it's impossible to come true. You have to be on "crack" to believe that it would either happen or that the characters wouldn't kill each other.

Kagema: are male prostitutes that usually take the role of an uke. You might find this word mostly in historical yaoi.

Rotten talk: is the conversations that fujoshi/fudanshi have when talking about BL. It can be as naive as just naming the ship they like, or as hot as heavy-fangirling on a yaoi manga.

Slash: is shipping characters of the same sex in fanfiction. This word can be used as a way to explain BL, and even as an equivalent. But it's mainly used in the realm of fanfiction.

Younger Seme: when the dominant in the couple is younger than the submissive partner.

SUB-GENRES IN BL

Arab: 「アラブ」 stories feature romances set in the dunes of the desert, with royalty, princes, kings, elite warriors, and oil multimillionaires. These stories don't depict reality at all. Instead, they show up an idealization of the Arabic world, and invented countries. People also call this sub-genre "stories of the dunes" 「砂漠もの」, although it's not a perfect synonym.

Exe-Kei/ Highso-Kei: 「エグゼ系／ハイソ系」 are stories about executives and the high society. The characters can be millionaires, bosses from a first class company, elite businessmen, gorgeous members of the high society, etc. Semes are the most common. However, you can also find ukes.

Gachimuchi: 「ガチムチ」 is a sub-genre where muscular men are king. Muscular, almost perfect men appear in the story. They tend to have the perfect body or show muscles that are about to burst. They can be young, or old, but they're usually very masculine.

Gakuenmono: 「学園もの」 is the King sub-genre in yaoi manga. It depicts bittersweet stories of young students and adolescents. Some live alone in boarding schools, and they struggle to fit in. Other stories are centered in characters that are members of the student council. Others depict students in clubs.

Gijinka: 「擬人化」 are stories about anthropomorphism. It means that animals, plants or things take the shape of a human. Imagine stories with dolls that come to life or animals. Although the ship looks human, the important part here is that it's more like someone is the plug, and someone else is the charger.

Jingai: 「人外」 means "not human." So, these stories are about humanoids, like robots. But, many times you can find characters with animal tails and ears. Many other times you can see the beasts as they're. So, they could be foxes, aliens, robots, etc.

Josou: 「女装」 means cross-dressing. This sub-genre features stories where a guy dresses like a woman because it might be his hobby, or it can be that the circumstances force him to crossdress. The cross-dresser is called "josou danshi" 「女装男子」 when it's just normal. But when he looks like a girl, then you use baby boy, "Otoko no ko" 「男の娘」. Both semes and ukes can be cross-dressers.

Omegaverse: 「オメガバース」 is an entire Universe where there're more genres than just male and female. Humans can also be alfa, beta or omega. Alfas are at the top of the social pyramid. They have all the best jobs, and they rule the world. Betas are just like you and me, and consider just "boring." And the omegas are in the lowest part of society. They can get pregnant, get uncontrollably hot once a month, and release strong feromones that seduce others. Because of that, they're regarded as inferior beings. There's been a boom in stories that are set in the Omegaverse. You can see a good correlation between the status of the omegas with women in society. Their problems at work, how people bully them, etc., are just problems that we can face too.

Otokomae: 「男前」 means handsome. These are stories where the characters are either handsome, or their actions are also handsome. There're both *semes* and *ukes*. However, in the case of the *uke*, it usually happens that they can lead a *seme*. So, think about stories where the characters are beautiful and are good-hearted.

Ry-man: 「リーマン」 are stories about businessmen. There's a fascination with the suit they wear. So, you can expect all types of panels with amazing men in incredible suits. The stories are also about bosses and their subordinates, the competition between colleagues, the relationship between trading partners, clients, etc. In many cases, these stories show us the sexual relationship in the working place.

Shota: 「ショタ」 is a sub-genre centered in young characters. They're around 15 years old. Frequently, there's only one young main character in the story, and the others are adults. *Shotas* can be pretty boys in boarding schools, energetic kids, or even evil ones. The stories usually feature the relationship between an adult and a minor. Some people also call this sub-genre *shotakon*.

StoM: 「SとM」 is just S&M. These stories are about the relationship between a dominant masochist *seme*, and a submissive *uke* that loves the deed. They explore the body in many ways, but also the mind.

Wanko: 「ワンコ」 are stories related to dogs, or dog-like characters. It might be their personality. So, imagine a story with someone who loves his partner so much, that he shakes his tail like a dog. Meaning, that he'll be with his partner faithfully whatever happens. Both *seme* and *uke* can have this character. It can also happen that one of them has a dog. You can also find stories with other types of pets, like cats or rabbits.

Yakuza: 「ヤクザ」 are stories about the Japanese mafia. Some main characters do look aggressive and fierce, others, however, are yakuza in disguise. These stories tend to be thrilling and very erotic. A good example is Finder, by Ayano Yamane. Asami is a fierce-looking yakuza. He's imposing, but he has a sweet spot for Akihito.

Yu-kakumono: 「遊郭もの」 are stories about prostitution and the red light district. They usually focus on a slim and petite *uke* who works in the red light district. The *uke* is constrained to sleep with many men, but he ends up falling in love with the *seme*. These stories can be very dramatic.

HONORABLE MENTIONS (II)

Ecchi/ Hentai: 「エッチ／ヘンタイ」 is a perverted sexual desire. Sometimes, in BL, characters might accuse someone of being H (read "ecchi") just because they're gay. This word is usually used in heterosexual porn, or when some character has some sort of fetish.

Hard Yaoi/ Hentai Yaoi: are stories with very graphic sex, or with intense BDSM, violence, or weird fetishes.

Okama: 「オカマ」 just means "gay." But it could be an insult, like "tranny," so beware of this word. It's usually used for men who dress like a woman. They might be or not transgender. You can find them in Secret XXX Peke Peke Peke, since one of the characters worked in a club cross-dressing.

MORE IN DEPTH

Today we're going to wrap up all the essential words in this guide to yaoi manga. I saved the juiciest for last, along with some honorable mentions that aren't that naughty. Most of the words refer to relationships between characters. Because most of the words are sex-related, I decided to hide them under a NSFW link. So, if you want to read them, please click on the NSFW link. You might find one word or many.

Ama-Ama: 「あまあま」 means "too sweet." It refers to couples that are very cheesy. You can even vomit sugar when all those lovely and cheesy feelings are exposed. You could end up vomiting sand if things get out of control. 「砂を吐く」 or, "suna wo haku."

Anany: 「アナニー」 is a compound word. Ana comes from hole, and "nany" from "onany," which means masturbation. An "anany" happens when a Uke uses his butt to get pleasure. It also happens when a Semi makes the Uke play with his own fingers. (Yes, I know, this list of words is very graphic!)

Bromance: 「ブロマンス」 is a compound word made by the words brother and romance. It's an extremely close relationship between two men, but it has no sex. If there's love, we have to take a look at the bromance case by case. If the bromance crosses the line, then we're talking about a ship.

Bukkake: 「ブッカケ」 is a hentai act that you might find in hard yaoi. It happens when a group of men come on the face (or body) of the Uke. It's a rare thing to find in a yaoi manga. But, if you read hard yaoi, you might end up reading such a scene.

Dry Orgasm: 「ドライオーガズム」 is just that. It happens when a Uke gets to the climax by getting aroused without ejaculating. It could happen by motivating the prostate gland by playing with it in different ways. A synonym for this is "mesuiki," 「メスイキ」.

Gekokujou: 「下克上」 is a relationship where an inferior attacks sexually a superior. It doesn't need to be violent. It can be that the subordinate is only approaching or flirting with the superior. It's a reversal of roles. Usually, you get a seme who is the boss. Here it's the uke who is ruling things. You can also find another expression: 「年下攻め」 "toshi shita seme."

Haramu: 「孕む」 happens when a man becomes pregnant despite being a man. It's a metaphor, but you can find it in the Omegaverse easily. Omegas can get pregnant regardless of their gender.

Ibutsusounyu: 「異物挿入」 means "to insert something alien." This happens when the Uke, or the Seme, introduces something alien in the Uke. By alien, I mean something else but the fingers or the genitals. It could be a sex toy, a banana, or even tentacles. Who knows, the Seme could be a shapeshifter!

Kaihatsu: 「開発」 us a development. In yaoi, it's when the Seme teaches the uke all about his body, including all the sexy bits about it. Well, especially those. If there's any kind of self-exploration, it's usually a type of training that the Seme imposes on the uke. There might also be sexual intercourse for the first time. Then, the exploration and development in discovering pleasure continues.

Kenkaple: 「ケンカップル」 is a couple that is fighting all the time. They're a "hate couple," and they end up being intimate because they fight a lot. If it goes out of hand, we're talking about a 「殴り愛」 "naguri ai" or a punching love.

Kyoudai: 「兄弟」 just means brothers. But in BL, we're talking about a romantic relationship between brothers. They can be brothers by blood, or by marriage. Despite being a forbidden relationship, love and desire flowers between them.

Kyouyuu: 「共有」 happens when two or more semes love the same uke. It can be just romantically, or also sexually. They share the Uke.

Nirinzashi: 「二輪挿し」 literally means "inserting two wheels." It happens when two Semes are inside a Uke at the same time. The wider the Uke gets, the wider the romance will get. Or so might think the Semes. But, some other characters might prefer exclusivity. In that case, we're talking about 「一棒一穴」 (hitobouhitoana) "one rod, one hole." Meaning that a single partner will devote himself to a single person.

Sand: 「サンド」 It's unlike a "friendly trio." It happens when there are a Uke, and two Semes that are in love with him. The ship's name is composed like this: "Seme x Uke x Seme."

Tokoroten: 「トコロテン」 happens when a Uke comes when the Seme penetrates him but doesn't touch his genitals (and the Uke doesn't touch them either). We can resume this action as "pushing and coming."

Yaoi Ana: 「やおい穴」 is an imaginary hole that's located between the male's genitals and the anus. Ukes usually have "yaoi ana." When they have sexual relationships, they use the "yaoi ana" instead of the anus (and many times, both). It also generates fluids as if it were a woman's. It's a little bit like unicorns and magic.

. . .

OTHER RELATED WORDS

Animix: 「アニミクス」 is an "almost anime." The only real animated feature is the characters mouths. Ayano Yamane's Finder has an animix. I bet they're far cheaper to create than a regular anime.

AV: or "adult video" refers to porn.

Cosname: 「コスネーム」 is the name that a person uses when cosplaying. Many cosplayers might use it as a way of disguise, especially if they're cosplaying BL characters.

Drama CD: 「ドラマCD」 is an audio performance of the yaoi manga. Many voice actors become famous and do have a fan base. You might even find short comics about the characters acting like the voice actors at the end of a manga, for example.

Doujinshi: 「同人誌」 are self-published works around a particular fandom. There are collections, art related to games, stories with characters of different anime, etc.

Host Club: 「ホストクラブ」 is a bar where male hosts will entertain women for the illusion of romance and sexual attraction. There are also host clubs with women serving men. Drinks are insanely expensive. Depending on the host club, workers are expected or not to accompany their clients out of the establishment. So, depending on the club, the rules are very different.

Light Novel: 「ライトノベル」 is a short novel with illustrations. They're usually series, and one-shots are rare. Many manga artists illustrate the light novels. They can be *yaoi* or not.

Otome Road: 「乙女ロード」 is the nickname of a road in Ikebukuro that's packed with shops that have items dedicated to a female audience. If you're searching for a *doujinshi*, odds are that you'll find the one you want there.

OVA: is an "original video animation." These aren't movies nor anime series. Instead, they explain something about the anime series. They can be a bridge between seasons or the explanation of a subplot.

Scanlation: is the process of scanning a manga, uploading it to a computer, and edit it to replace the Japanese for the translation. It's a very long process, and many people might be working for such a page to exist somewhere online.

Scanlator: is a manga-lover that decides to *scanlate* manga, edit it, and then translate it. It can be that it's a group of *scanlators* to do all the job.

Tankoubon: 「単行本」 is a volume that collects different chapters of manga. It usually has manga that has already been published before, or it's a collection of one-shots.

Tsundere: 「ツンデレ」 is a character that looks cold, or that gets angry very quickly. However, they do so because they're shy or get embarrassed easily. Inside they're super soft beings.

Yandere: 「ヤンデレ」 are characters that are obsessive, and entirely in love with someone to the point of being sick. Their actions can come as "too much."

ABOUT DEPEPI

MEET THE AUTHOR

Pepi is an experienced writer, geek entrepreneur, intrepid adventurer and daring creative based in Brighton, the UK. DePepi is where she showcases her expertise, shares ideas, reviews, and thoughts about movies, series, books, fandoms, and all things pop culture. Thanks to the interaction with the Geek community she dared to share beyond what she thought possible giving back as many positive vibes as possible.

She's passionate about learning languages and discovering new pop culture outlets, venturing into new fantasy worlds and exploring where creativity can bring you.

She's lived more than eight years in Japan and traveled solo with her backpack in Europe, Australia and New Zealand. After some rocky adventures in love, career and life, she can honestly say that this is just the beginning 😌

instagram.com/depepi

Join dePepi's Newsletter and get all the news and tips to ignite your writing:

Join the Fun!

Receive news once or twice a month :)

Collect the details you need to stay in touch.

Email Address

First Name

https://mailchi.mp/8ffb26f0daa5/join-the-fun

Love sharing steamy stories? Join the new forums and get access to all courses as well! (Yaoi, writing, Tarot… and Pepi's old very questionable writings!)

https://www.depepi.com

Use the code DEPEPILOVE when subscribing to a WordSmith subscription for a £1.99 the first month, £3.99 from the second month after (valid until March 26th 2025)